IF I LIVE

(A Ruby Hunter Mystery—Book 3)

Molly Black

Molly Black

Bestselling author Molly Black is author of the MAYA GRAY FBI suspense thriller series, comprising nine books (and counting); of the RYLIE WOLF FBI suspense thriller series, comprising six books; of the TAYLOR SAGE FBI suspense thriller series, comprising eight books; of the KATIE WINTER FBI suspense thriller series, comprising eleven books (and counting); of the RUBY HUNTER FBI suspense thriller series, comprising five books (and counting); of the CAITLIN DARE FBI suspense thriller series, comprising five books (and counting); and of the REESE LINK mystery series, comprising five books (and counting).

An avid reader and lifelong fan of the mystery and thriller genres, Molly loves to hear from you, so please feel free to visit www.mollyblackauthor.com to learn more and stay in touch.

ISBN: 978-1-0943-7849-7

BOOKS BY MOLLY BLACK

MAYA GRAY MYSTERY SERIES
GIRL ONE: MURDER (Book #1)
GIRL TWO: TAKEN (Book #2)
GIRL THREE: TRAPPED (Book #3)
GIRL FOUR: LURED (Book #4)
GIRL FIVE: BOUND (Book #5)
GIRL SIX: FORSAKEN (Book #6)
GIRL SEVEN: CRAVED (Book #7)
GIRL EIGHT: HUNTED (Book #8)
GIRL NINE: GONE (Book #9)

RYLIE WOLF FBI SUSPENSE THRILLER
FOUND YOU (Book #1)
CAUGHT YOU (Book #2)
SEE YOU (Book #3)
WANT YOU (Book #4)
TAKE YOU (Book #5)
DARE YOU (Book #6)

TAYLOR SAGE FBI SUSPENSE THRILLER
DON'T LOOK (Book #1)
DON'T BREATHE (Book #2)
DON'T RUN (Book #3)
DON'T FLINCH (Book #4)
DON'T REMEMBER (Book #5)
DON'T TELL (Book #6)

KATIE WINTER FBI SUSPENSE THRILLER
SAVE ME (Book #1)
REACH ME (Book #2)
HIDE ME (Book #3)
BELIEVE ME (Book #4)
HELP ME (Book #5)
FORGET ME (Book #6)

HOLD ME (Book #7)
PROTECT ME (Book #8)
REMEMBER ME (Book #9)
CATCH ME (Book #10)
WATCH ME (Book #11)

RUBY HUNTER FBI SUSPENSE THRILLER
IF I RUN (Book #1)
IF I TELL (Book #2)
IF I LIVE (Book #3)
IF I FORGET (Book #4)
IF I RETURN (Book #5)

CAITLIN DARE FBI SUSPENSE THRILLER
COME GET ME (Book #1)
COME FIND ME (Book #2)
COME TAKE ME (Book #3)
COME CATCH ME (Book #4)
COME SAVE ME (Book #5)

REESE LINK MYSTERY
BEYOND REASON (Book #1)
BEYOND REACH (Book #2)
BEYOND REPAIR (Book #3)
BEYOND DOUBT (Book #4)
BEYOND NORMAL (Book #5)

PROLOGUE

Daisy Hauser swiped the Sky Guide app off her phone's screen and checked her text messages again. Still nothing. She nervously nipped at the nail on her middle finger, wondering if Harrison had gotten tied up at work.

She looked at her last text with Harrison and smiled. They had only been dating three weeks, but he already felt like home. Daisy wasn't quick to call it love, but everything was different with Harrison. Maybe love is exactly what it was.

A brisk wind whipped her chestnut hair off her neck for a moment before rolling through the trees behind her. She pulled her jacket tighter to ward off the chill. Daisy didn't mind the cold, especially when she would have Harrison to keep her warm.

Daisy looked up at the stars. Orion's Lookout was the perfect spot for stargazing, something she and Harrison both loved. It was one of the many interests they had in common. She could see Orion's Belt perfectly, along with so many others, from the rock she'd picked out. Normally, it was hard to see the stars with a full moon, but Orion's Lookout was like a little nest surrounded by sky-reaching pine trees. The moon hadn't reached its apex yet, which meant they still had time to see the stars.

It was a clear night, one of the first they had had in a while. Harrison had told her about Orion's Lookout on their third date. She'd always heard of it as a "lover's lane" kind of place, so she'd never had much of a reason to go. Then he'd told her about all the amazing constellations and comets he'd seen. It seemed like the perfect spot for a late-night picnic.

The wicker basket next to her was filled to the brim with all of their favorite finger foods and sweets. She'd made cucumber sandwiches, spinach artichoke dip, homemade pita bread, peanut butter fudge, and lemon blueberry scones. She'd thrown several ice packs in to keep everything fresh and topped off the basket with two mason jars of sweet tea.

The trailhead was about fifty yards from the clearing, but the hike was slippery and steep in spots. The basket wasn't heavy on flat ground, but she definitely struggled carrying it all the way from the car. A couple she passed on the way up had even offered to help even though they were leaving. She was glad Harrison hadn't seen her trying to lug the basket, a blanket, and her purse all by herself. Daisy had no doubt it would have made him laugh, which made her chuckle too.

Her body thrummed with excitement to see him again. She checked the time on her phone. It was almost midnight. He was late . . . and technically, she was trespassing. Daisy looked around, unsure if anyone patrolled the area after dark. Hopefully, Harrison would be there to calm her fears, soon. It was one thing to trespass with someone she liked to see this perfect view of the stars. It was something completely different to get stood up *and* get caught breaking the law.

The wind had died down, and whatever wildlife there was around her was quiet. Daisy saw the outlines of trees against the slightly light sky, and she noticed how still everything was. A chill crept up her spine.

She heard a car door shut in the distance and what she thought might be footsteps. Her heart hammered with anticipation. She pulled several battery-operated votives out of her purse and set them around the picnic basket. It was darker than she'd expected, and she didn't want Harrison to miss her surprise.

She flicked each votive on and turned toward the hiking trail with a bright smile. Daisy's eyes struggled to adjust to the darkness at the other end of the clearing.

"Harrison?"

No answer.

Daisy's breath hitched in her throat. A tall, broad-shouldered man was running right at her. She searched his face, trying to make sense of what was happening and who he was. Every cell in her body froze instantly like the temperature had just dropped to zero degrees.

His long gait brought him closer and closer. Daisy launched herself from the rock with all the strength she had. She darted to the left, just as he reached for her. Narrowly missing his grasp, she heard the man crash into the rock with a thud. She willed her legs to run faster than she ever had. Daisy was not a runner, but in this moment, she was willing to do anything necessary to escape this stranger.

The trail opening was only a few yards ahead. Her shins burned almost as badly as her lungs as she pushed herself harder toward safety. *Just a few more steps.*

Then she heard it. Another car door shutting in the distance. *Harrison.* But that wasn't all she heard. Footsteps running behind her drowned her hope in an instant. *He's too close.* Daisy summoned every iota of strength she had to scream. Someone else was there. Someone else would hear.

She opened her mouth just as a large hand clamped around her throat, silencing her. She punched and kicked at shadows, doing her best to stay upright. Suddenly, her back slammed against the ground, knocking her breath and the fight out of her. She immediately tried to get up, but it was like a boulder had been rolled on top of her.

Daisy shoved and wriggled beneath the weight, desperate to be free. Her voice failed her, but she would not stop trying to get away. She bucked and swung as hard as she could. She felt what she was sure was hair brush her right hand. Daisy grabbed until she caught a handful and yanked as hard as she could. The attacker groaned, giving her just enough strength to try to get away one more time.

She shoved the weight of him off her and scrambled to her feet. But before she could take another step toward freedom, she felt a thick rope wrap around her neck.

Daisy Hauser never had a chance.

CHAPTER ONE

Ruby! Wait! I can't keep up!

FBI Agent Ruby Hunter was haunted by last words. Those were just some of them.

The voice of her childhood best friend, Geri, called to her, just as loudly as it had that day.

No, even louder, now.

Because now it felt like there was a tie to an even bigger mystery, one that had already consumed most of her life.

As Ruby drove north on the highway, she looked over at the thin file in her passenger seat. It was a case file for Geraldine Forge's disappearance. Pathetic and thin, it contained very little information, simply because there'd been very little information. *Without a trace,* the police and media had said, again and again. No leads. No suspects. Nothing. It was as if the earth had opened up and swallowed the little girl—and her red bicycle—whole.

Someone had slipped the file in with the Vallejo case files. Someone who had access to her and who knew she was connected to the missing girl. *Geri.* Her childhood friend who'd disappeared, still yet to be found.

Eventually, Geri's bicycle was found in a muddy ditch, about a half a mile from her home. Ruby still remembered the flyers she'd attached to every lamppost in town. The image of Geri's ever-smiling face staring back at her every time she'd tacked up another flyer was seared into her brain like some sort of trauma brand.

But there were other last words, like the words of her dead partner and lover, Asher Carnes, had written just days before he was brutally murdered by Vincent Vallejo, over three years ago.

He always has something to say. He wants us to realize how smart he is.

Asher had been the thirteenth victim of one of the nation's most notorious serial killers. Or so everyone believed.

She'd solved two new cases in recent months where the serial killers used aspects of Vallejo's murders.

But there were six more women she didn't save.

Somehow, copycats Jared Reuben and Aaron Rodney knew details from Vallejo's murders that had never been shared with the public and that only a handful of FBI agents knew. The killers didn't have any known connections to each other, and they hadn't found any concrete proof they had recently been in contact with Vallejo.

At first, Ruby could not believe Vallejo had anything to do with the murders. He was in solitary confinement. He'd had no visitors except Ruby, and that had only happened twice since he'd been caught more than three years ago. The warden at Boone Correctional Facility, Percy Woodward, had assured Ruby that all communications in and out had been stopped. Vallejo had zero contact with the outside world.

Ruby had solved each of the two new cases based on her extensive knowledge of the Lucky 13 murders, her first big case as a BAU profiler. It was knowledge she wished every day she didn't have. But she'd also had help. Vincent Vallejo, Lucky 13 himself, had given her the clues she needed to find the killers. They were wrapped in misdirection and riddles, of course, but he'd still helped her. Ruby hated with every fiber of her being that she hadn't been able to solve the Reuben and Rodney case without him.

She didn't know how Vallejo was pulling the strings from solitary, but she was ready to find out. It was hard for her to believe he had that kind of power, but she simply could not think of anyone else who had the savvy. He was always strategizing, always fifteen steps ahead of everyone else.

Ruby thought of Asher, and how that night, the last night she saw him, they'd talked about the mind games the killer was playing with them. With Asher. He'd brought Chinese over to discuss the case, but they hadn't done much eating, or discussing. No, they'd gone straight to bed. He'd been so serious, so absorbed in finding Vallejo, and she'd wanted to ease those worries he seemed to carry on his back like an albatross. She'd wanted to help him.

But she'd been no help at all, it turned out. As a partner, or as a lover.

She'd been so naïve, so lovestruck by him, her first real relationship, that even work fell by the wayside. Ruby now believed Vallejo depended on the distraction and used it against them.

That night, they'd made plans to tell Bellisario, the Deputy Director, about their relationship—to lay it all out on the table and make it official. Ruby had fallen asleep in the arms of the man she loved, trusting their lives together were only going to get better.

But then Asher had gotten a call, a witness who wanted to meet up, and he'd rushed from bed in the middle of the night. She'd never even gotten a chance to say goodbye. Sometimes, it felt like she was waking up that next morning all over again, her bed empty and her phone buzzing. Vallejo had texted her an address from Asher's phone. She'd thought it was from Asher, that he'd gotten a lead.

Instead, Ruby had been the one who found Asher's mutilated body. He'd been tortured and left for dead like a piece of garbage. It was one of the many gruesome images Ruby carried with her, and unfortunately, the last one she had of Asher aside from the FBI portrait they had on an easel at his funeral.

He's playing a game with me. He knows things about me. Things I have never told anyone.

Asher had said those words about Vallejo to Ruby the night she lost him. He'd told her he'd gotten some text messages from an unknown number, taunting him with bits and pieces of information no one else could possibly know. Ruby remembered the conversation as if it had just happened.

"What kind of information, Asher? Like work stuff or personal stuff?" she'd asked one night as they shared a bottle of wine in front of the television.

"It's not about the information. It's about how the information is being used. This person is trying to throw me off my game, put me on edge."

"So, let's talk it through like we do with everything else. Once we know the players, we might know who's messing with you."

Instead of sharing his secrets with her, he'd taken her to bed. She hadn't minded the change of subject, but she'd intended to follow up with him the next day. She just never got the chance.

Ruby shook the memory from her mind and focused on the road ahead. She knew Vallejo was playing some sort of sick, twisted game, but she didn't know the rules or how to win. After the last case, Ruby understood anyone could have fallen under Vallejo's spell. She'd hoped the Aaron Rodney case was the end of it, but everything in her bones told her it wasn't. Now, it was time to talk to Vallejo, again.

The Boone Correctional Facility in Eastern Maryland was just as stark and imposing as it had been during Ruby's first visit to see Vallejo. As she drove the familiar roads from Quantico, it loomed ahead of her, daunting. It was the haunted house she'd refused to go in as a child, the never-changing place all her nightmares came true.

Warden Percy Woodward had made it his priority to escort Ruby to see Vallejo whenever she visited. It was as if he wanted to personally assure her that Vallejo was under lock and key, the utmost scrutiny. Ruby knew better. They both did.

Percy Woodward was a thin man, someone with more of an academic and bureaucratic air than that of a bully. In the chaos of a place like Boone Correctional Facility, Woodward's even-tempered and strait-laced presence was the perfect public façade, a calming, rational face on such a brutal interior.

And it was brutal. As the only maximum-security prison in the state, Boone Correctional Facility housed only the worst of the worst.

But one wouldn't know it, talking to Woodward. He spoke of his prisoners in such a humane

way, as if they were residents of a nursing home, instead of cruel monsters convicted of the worst crimes humanly possible.

His voice was pleasant and singsong, relaxed in comparison to his stiff, blue-gray suit, melding with the bland halls. His sharp cheekbones caught the harsh lighting, casting deep shadows on his pale face. Ruby wondered if his life had become parallel with the lives of the prisoners, always indoors away from the sun.

As they walked the bleak hallway, the warden said, "Mr. Vallejo wasn't surprised when we told him he had a visitor. He was *enthusiastic* to see you again, more so than I think I've ever seen him."

Ruby frowned. "You didn't tell him I was coming," she said, her gut twisting.

"You know as well as I do. No one has to tell him anything, Special Agent Hunter. He always seems to know, just like last time. Only we can't figure out how. He has no comms in or out. I personally made sure of it."

Superhuman.

Ruby was sick of the word floating into her consciousness every time it seemed Vallejo had managed to do the impossible. He was just a man. He was intelligent, cunning, and perceptive, but he was still only a man. Flesh and blood, a heartbeat, and a brain. Ruby repeated these words to herself as they reached the door.

"Let me know if you need anything," Woodward said. She nodded as the accompanying guard unlocked and opened the door. She inhaled a deep, calming breath. It was important she appeared confident and unshakeable in front of Vallejo.

Before Ruby could cross the threshold, her phone buzzed on her hip.

"Sorry, just a moment." Ruby stepped back and lifted the phone to her ear as the guard closed the door, waiting for her cue.

"Hunter," she answered without looking at the number.

"Special Agent Hunter, where are you?" Ruby froze at the sound of FBI Executive Assistant Director Barrett Murphy's demanding baritone.

"Sir, I just …"

"Think hard before you lie to me, Hunter."

"Sir …?"

Ruby wasn't a good liar. Asher had caught her in every lie she'd told him, even the innocent ones. He'd finally taken her aside and told her lying was never going to be her strong suit. It wasn't a bad thing, but it definitely could be an obstacle for an agent in the FBI if criminals always knew when she wasn't telling the truth. Asher had looked her straight in the eyes and told her, "Don't lie. Omit. You'll be a lot more successful."

"Sir, I have some errands I need to take care of this morning, and I already cleared it with Deputy Director Bellisario. Was there something you needed?"

She *was* running some errands before coming into work, just one of those errands happened to be visiting a convicted murderer at a maximum-security prison.

Ruby knew dropping the Deputy Director's name wasn't going to win her any points with Barrett Murphy, but at least it would get him off her back.

"What did I tell you about Vallejo?" he asked, as if she was a toddler who'd been told to keep her hand out of a cookie jar.

Ruby was literally steps away from the man, and she wasn't going to leave without seeing Vallejo. She didn't know what Murphy's problem was, but he always seemed to have something to say to her.

Ruby had to think fast on her feet. "I'm sorry, sir, you're breaking up … what was that? Hello? Are you still there?"

Ruby caught the guard watching her, a smirk on his face like he knew that she was totally lying to whomever was on the phone. She felt the heat of embarrassment flush her face and turned her back to the man.

"Special Agent Hunter, you better be at your desk in thirty minutes or else …"

"Sir, it's a really bad connection. If you can hear me, I'll be in soon." Ruby ended the call before she had to listen to another word of that man berating her. Any confidence she'd mustered before taking Murphy's call had withered to dust.

Barrett Murphy had never been a team player. He had been promoted to the Executive Assistant Director of the BAU two years ago, but the job he really wanted was Bellisario's. Murphy thought he could do everything better than Bellisario, better than everyone else. No one agreed with his self-assessment on any level.

Murphy was a spoiled DC kid who'd had every door opened to him just because he was born a Murphy. To the average person, Barrett Murphy was a nobody. In the world of Intelligence, he was the scion of a sitting US Senator and a retired Federal Judge, both of whom had had storied careers at the CIA and FBI respectively. His mother, Senator Melinda Murphy, also led the US Senate Select Committee on Intelligence, a position that only helped her son further his standing at the Bureau. After all, in DC, politics and pedigree were every bit as important as solving cases.

Barrett Murphy had had it out for Ruby ever since she cracked the Vallejo case. He'd even tried to have her suspended for not following protocol when she apprehended Vallejo, but Bellisario had stopped him at every turn.

Asher had always referred to Barrett Murphy as a "man-child," someone to mostly be ignored. He didn't live long enough to see the monster he'd become. The more success Ruby had, the more impossible it was to ignore him. He acted like she'd taken something from him, but just *what,* she didn't know.

All she knew was that he was going to try to do everything possible to ruin her.

But that particular worry could wait, for right now.

She pocketed her phone and looked at the guard. "Sorry. I'm ready."

CHAPTER TWO

Ruby entered the room, hoping she'd be more comfortable this time. The third time's a charm, or so they said.

She didn't feel charmed in the least.

Vincent Vallejo sat at the familiar metal table in a small, austere room. It was bolted to the floor, and he was chained to it, somewhere below. She'd heard the clank of the chains once before when he'd adjusted in the chair, causing the chains to rattle. Ruby had immediately understood his adjustment was just for her, him wanting her to feel some sense of safety in his presence. It seemed important to him to make her comfortable, lure her into thinking he couldn't get to her while he was locked up behind these walls.

Ruby noticed Vallejo rarely moved. He didn't fidget, or jump, or fix his clothing. He calculated every gesture as he calculated everything else. He likely knew the exact moment the door would open, because his expression was serene and pleasant every time.

During Vallejo's trial, the public struggled to believe this handsome, charismatic man had violently murdered thirteen people. The trial was televised, which only made his fandom grow. Women and men alike stood outside the courthouse daily, desperately waiting to get just a glimpse of him. It was disgusting the amount of adulation he inspired.

Ruby put Murphy out of her mind and focused on Vallejo. Handsome as always, he had sharp features like he'd been carved from stone by some Renaissance hand. His jumpsuit was neat and well-pressed, like it had been made for him by a Savile Row. He had a way of elevating the outfit, making it look as dignified as a three-piece suit.

She'd noted the last time she'd visited that he was thinner and paler than he was when she put him here, but he still held himself like the distinguished professor he once was. Ruby wondered if he missed being outside, being able to do what he wanted when he wanted. He seemed too comfortable, like being locked up in a maximum-security prison was just a change of geography, nothing more.

As Ruby lowered herself into a chair across from Vallejo, she thought of the moment she'd seen him in the courtroom. On that last day, she'd had to take the stand to relay the details of the investigation and, in particular, Asher's death. Somehow, she'd managed to do so emotionlessly, as if she'd just read about him in a case file rather than lived those horrible days herself.

She'd refused to make eye contact with him while the world watched her share grisly and gruesome details of each murder. She'd looked in his general direction when appropriate but never into the ice-blue eyes watching her now.

"Special Agent Hunter. How lovely to see you again. Don't you just look as fresh as a daisy."

Vallejo's voice made her stomach coil into a tight knot. She loathed the way he acted like she *wanted* to be there. She'd rather be anywhere else, but she could not deny he'd helped her. He'd given her *just enough* in a sea of nonsense, a test to see if she would sink or swim.

She despised the fact that the very same monster who'd snuffed out the lives of so many was the one person who seemed to be able to help her when she'd had no leads on the last two cases. She knew he was playing some kind of game with her, but she wasn't sure if it was purely just for his enjoyment or something more. With Vallejo, it seemed like it was always something more.

After the last case, Ruby was tired of always being behind, always racing to the scene and hoping she was going to get there in time. Dana Jacobson and Maureen Fantasia were alive because of Ruby and her new partner, Gabe Ruiz, but also because of the hints Vallejo had given her.

This time, she'd come to see Vallejo *before* the murders started. When she told Gabe her plan, he warned her that she was wasting her time, that Vallejo wouldn't talk to her. He liked the urgency that came with multiple deaths, the desperation Ruby had every time she couldn't seem to find a way forward. Gabe swore up and down that even if Vallejo did talk to her, he wouldn't give her anything tangible. Ruby hoped he was wrong, but she had to try something different. She had to try to get ahead.

And the one thing about Gabe Ruiz was that he wasn't blind. He'd also started to see the patterns and how Vallejo knew more than he should for a prisoner in solitary confinement. He couldn't explain how the killers knew the details they did, but he refused to believe that Vincent Vallejo was some kind of mastermind with a grand scheme of murder and mayhem.

He's not some kind of comic book villain, Ruby. He's just a man, and he's going to spend the rest of his life in prison.

Ruby knew in her gut that Vallejo was involved but thinking of Gabe's words settled her just enough to meet Vallejo eye-to-eye.

"This isn't a social visit."

"I believe that would depend on your perspective. Wouldn't you agree?"

To Ruby's ears, it sounded like a taunt. No one else would hear it the same way, though. Even if she recorded it and replayed it for an audience, he'd still seem as polite and innocent as ever. But Ruby knew better.

Vallejo had never been the kind of man who asked questions unless he already knew the answer.

He knows things about me. Things I have never told anyone.

Ruby pushed Asher's words from her mind and tried to focus on the monster in front of her wearing a skin suit. There was no doubt in her mind that Vallejo took the utmost pleasure in this. Maximum-security prison was not exactly known for its wealth of entertainment. What could please him more than Ruby, of all people, coming to visit?

Ruby's nerve endings tingled with anxiety and rage. It annoyed her to think she was a source of amusement or even joy. She glared at Vallejo. It would be so easy to snap his neck. Her eyes drifted to his throat for just a moment. Vallejo smiled as if he knew exactly what she was thinking.

"I wanted to tell you face-to-face, your angel, Bezaliel, didn't make it."

Vallejo smirked. "Another case solved, Hunter. You're starting to make quite a name for yourself. First me, then two more. You're on a roll. Your parents must be so proud."

Ruby bristled at his comment. She knew he knew more about her than he should. He knew about the trailer she'd grown up in, even used it as a clue to help her find Dana Jacobson before Jared Reuben could killer her too.

He knows things about me.

Ruby was trying so hard not to let him get to her. For once, she wanted to get under *his* skin, not the other way around. She steadied her breathing and forced herself into stillness. She focused on the cold metal of the chair instead of Asher's words or Vallejo's provocations.

"I also wanted to share that Maureen's going to make a full recovery from yet another bungled attempt on her life."

Ruby watched Vallejo for micro expressions or movements that would belie his cool façade. She immediately noticed his jaw clench hard enough to shift his cheeks the tiniest amount. Just once. Just enough for her to know she'd landed a blow.

One thing I absolutely do detest is unfinished business.

He'd said it himself. Ruby wondered if he'd goaded her with his riddles because he didn't believe she would solve them in time, that she would fail and have even more blood on her hands than she already did. Or maybe she was a pawn in a game she had no idea how to play, and he was testing her to see how far she would go to save the day.

"How wonderful for Ms. Fantasia. Evil thwarted in the nick of time. It's a shame you weren't able to do the same for Special Agent Carnes."

Vallejo wielded his words expertly, cutting her to the bone. He knew Ruby couldn't have saved Asher; he planned it that way. The medical examiner even confirmed Asher had been dead for more than thirty minutes when the text was sent from his phone, proving there was nothing anyone could've done to keep Asher Carnes from dying.

Vallejo also knew she blamed herself. She wore Asher Carnes's death like a funeral shroud every day. She hated that he could see right through her, see her open wounds and scars so easily.

Ruby shifted slightly in her seat, struggling to stay calm, to sit across from this man who'd taken so much from her. From so many. She wanted him to suffer, to permanently wipe that smug look off his face and make him feel real pain. But he always seemed to have the upper hand.

But what was the end game? What was the point of any of this? She decided to take a different approach. Every time she was in front of him, she did her best to show strength and courage. But he saw her as weak, inept. Maybe she should act that way, see what kind of response it solicited.

"I know I didn't outsmart you or win whatever game you were playing."

"It's your name on the arrest warrant, is it not?"

"I may have been the one who brought you in, but anybody's name could've been on the paperwork."

"I'm afraid we must agree to disagree. Your name was the only name that was ever going to be on my paperwork."

Ruby laughed at his word choice. She doubted Vallejo had ever been afraid of anything in his life. She could see how much he was enjoying this dialogue. It disgusted her that she was entertaining him.

"I'm no genius, but even I can see you're only here because you want to be. One of your followers said as much."

"Aren't we all where we want to be, Special Agent Hunter?" Vallejo tsked. "And how do you know you're not a genius? Have you been tested?"

"Besides by you?"

Vallejo's face filled with a cunning grin like a Cheshire cat.

Ruby wasn't trying to be funny. Her expression remained unchanged.

Vallejo shifted in his seat, forcing the chains to clank below the table. His smile slowly dissolved into a flat line.

"While your visits are always welcome, I'd hate for anyone to get the wrong idea about us."

Ruby scoffed. She hoped *no one* would ever confuse her with a lovestruck groupie.

"Don't flatter yourself. I am only here to find out what you have planned," she hissed. Satisfaction lit up his face like a firework. He knew he was winning. He always seemed to be winning in this imaginary game of his.

"The last two times you were here, you left before we'd finished talking. Some might consider that to be rude, Special Agent Hunter." His words scolded her, but his tone was neutral. "Although, at least last time you brought your sense of humor with you."

Ruby never liked to use the word "hate," but she knew without any doubt that she hated this man with every fiber of her being. He never let her forget any misstep, any miscalculation. The last time she was in a room with Vallejo, she'd gotten so angry with him toying with her that she'd lost her cool. The only impact her outburst had on him was sheer delight. She would not make that mistake again.

"I'm not here to make friends, Vallejo. I am here for answers."

"Well, Special Agent Hunter, as you know, I have got all the time in the world." He smiled warmly at her, like his multiple life sentences meant nothing. Ruby knew the sad truth. That's exactly what they meant to him: nothing.

After all, Vallejo was only here because he *allowed* the FBI, *Ruby*, to catch him.

"What kinds of signs are you sending your followers to trigger the killings?" It was a bold question, but she had to try. Asher would've considered it sloppy, but Ruby didn't care. Thanks to Vallejo, Asher wasn't here to tell her what to do anymore.

Ruby glanced quickly at the clock behind Vallejo. She could not keep this up for much longer. Barrett Murphy had no doubt called Bellisario by now to see if she was at her desk. Hopefully, the Deputy Director still had her back when it came to her unorthodox methods.

"Signs? How can I send signs from solitary?" he ruminated.

"I saw you with the newspaper, Vallejo." Ruby cut directly to the chase. She needed him to tell her something, *anything*, she could use to get ahead.

"I'd hardly call the *Life and Style* section from several weeks ago anything to write home about. Speaking of home, how are Doug and Carole? Are they *frantic* with worry every time they see their darling girl in the headlines?"

"Not at all. They're proud. To them, serial killers are sickos that need to be eliminated." Ruby could hear Asher in her head sighing at her feeble attempt to lie. But it wasn't entirely a lie. It was more like wishful thinking.

"What are serial killers to you?"

"Bottom-feeders with zero purpose."

Vallejo's ice-blue eyes flashed with irritation for only a moment, long enough for Ruby to know she'd landed another blow. It was a small hit, but it was something.

Like so many before him, Vallejo believed his murders were the result of a higher calling, a divine purpose the pedestrian and uninspired could never understand. To Ruby, he was just another psychopath with a god complex.

Serenity washed over him before she could truly relish in the little victory. "While many strangers may aim to imitate my work, Special Agent Hunter, as I told you before, *my work is done*. And as much as I'd love to keep you *tied up* here a little longer, I believe you are due back at the office."

Ruby froze. He must have overheard her conversation with Murphy. He knew she was on borrowed time before she even sat down. Yet again, he was so many steps ahead of her, and she didn't even have a clue.

"You're right. I do have better things to do than listen to some old man's nonsense." She stood up and slid the chair back into place in one move. Ruby's insults were childish, but she suspected by the great care Vallejo took in his appearance that he was at least a little vain. And vanity for most was the weakest link in the chain of their ego.

Ruby turned her back to Vallejo, walked to the cell door, and knocked for the guard to let her out. She hated waiting for the door to open, for her to get to a space where she wasn't breathing the same air as this monster.

"Maybe next time you can bring the *new* Special Agent Carnes with you. That is, of course, if he's still around," he called out as the door opened. It took every ounce of strength Ruby had to walk across the threshold as if his words didn't slice right through her as he intended. Gabe was right. It had been a mistake to come here. Again.

Ruby took a deep breath of fresh air as she stepped outside the walls of the Boone Correctional Facility. Vallejo knew *exactly* how to wound her up with the least amount of effort. She swallowed the lump in her throat and headed for her car. Her phone buzzed just as she sat down in the driver's seat.

Headquarters.

"Hunter," she answered, praying it wasn't Murphy.

But it was the voice of Deputy Director Bellisario. "How fast can you get here? We've got another one."

CHAPTER THREE

Ruby checked her phone as she stepped onto the elevator back at headquarters. Almost noon.

She had completely wasted her entire morning with Vallejo, not to mention likely gotten herself in hot water with Murphy. He'd explicitly told her to stay away from Vallejo, that she was compromising the Bureau by consulting with a convicted serial killer. Ruby knew she'd done no such thing. Murphy just couldn't stand that no matter how much he tried to impede her career, she continued to thrive.

And for what? She hadn't even begun to find a connection between Vallejo and her childhood best friend, Geri. Was there even one? Or was it just him toying with her again?

She gritted her teeth. Stupid, thinking Vallejo would do anything more than toy with her. All she'd wanted was some small clue about what was coming next. She wanted to believe the cases were over, that Vallejo's work really was done. But her gut told her there were more out there like Jared Reuben and Aaron Rodney. She didn't know if this new case was also one of Vallejo's followers, but she knew going forward that that was always going to be something she'd have to rule out.

Ruby sucked in a deep breath, doing her best to silence the recriminations that seemed to play on a constant loop in her head. She'd failed to save Asher. She'd failed to bring true justice to Vallejo. She'd failed to get a single bit of direction from Vallejo and risked her career for nothing.

Serial killers are like weeds. You pull one up, and two more sprout up in its place.

Ruby's mother's words had been more accurate than she knew, only it might not just be two sprouting up in Vallejo's place. It could be an infinite amount.

The sickness, it spreads.

The elevator dinged, and the doors opened. Gabe was waiting for her. This time, he didn't jump out at her. Instead, he leaned against a desk with his arms crossed. Athletic and tan, a broad-shouldered Latino, Gabe Ruiz rarely stood still.

His eyes drifted to his watch and back to her.

"I know, I know," she said as she threw her things down on the desk. She put her hands up in a stopping motion, warning him not to give her any grief. "I came as soon as I heard."

"Yeah, something about another murder. But there's more. Bellisario's been on the phone for the last hour. Something about Murphy?"

Ruby's stomach filled with dread. The only good thing about her coming back to the FBI is that she didn't have to report directly to Murphy. She was there at Bellisario's personal request, and that was one of her stipulations. She knew the trouble he could make for her, and she was not about to have to clear every single decision with him. It was also probably the only reason she was still an active agent and not on desk duty.

"Ruiz! Hunter! Get in here!" Bellisario shouted as he slammed down the phone. Ruby was surprised he didn't break it. She looked at Gabe, curious about his reaction. He seemed to feel the same sense of bewilderment that she did.

Warren Bellisario rarely lost his temper, let alone raised his voice. Ruby watched as he paced furiously behind his desk, his face red and his hands pulling at his tie like he was trying to loosen it for more air. She knew he was likely counting to ten, or one hundred and ten, to calm himself down enough to keep their discussion professional. He was nothing if not professional, but she'd also never seen him this worked up.

Bellisario didn't have the same bureaucratic air about him that most people in management often did. Unlike some of his predecessors, he had once been an agent. He understood the politics of his position, but he also understood the perspective of those with their feet on the ground. It's what made him good at his job.

Ruby waited to speak. She had rarely seen Bellisario mad, and she didn't want to make things worse. Gabe started to say something, but she caught his eye first. She slightly shook her head, warning him to keep his mouth shut. He gave her an annoyed look and redirected his attention to Bellisario.

It took almost a full minute for Bellisario to pace himself into a better headspace. Ruby wished that worked for her, but Vallejo had ripped all her scabs off with just a few words. She felt like her wounds were oozing and now completely exposed for anyone to see.

Bellisario took his seat and assessed the two of them. "Did you get anything from Vallejo, Special Agent Hunter?" He clasped his hands and rested them in front of him.

"Nothing solid." Ruby looked away, unable to bear the thought of sharing even a second of her humiliation with them.

"Here." Bellisario slid three case files forward. "We already have three victims. The most recent is from approximately three weeks ago."

"How are we just now hearing about these?" Ruiz asked, just as dumbfounded as Ruby was.

"They're in different states. Virginia, Maryland, and Ohio. We haven't found any connections between the victims yet, but we're one hundred percent sure it's the same unsub."

"How?" Ruby blurted out. She felt her cheeks redden at her eagerness. It didn't matter how they knew. All that mattered was that they had another serial killer on their hands. The third one in less than a year.

Bellisario didn't answer right away. Ruby's mind went into overdrive. *Please don't let this be tied to Vallejo,* she pleaded in her head. She understood his reach, how he very likely had some kind of vile cult of killers out there . . . but she wasn't sure she could last through another one.

"The murder weapon for each victim was a four-foot piece of rope. Each rope was handmade with the same thirteen threads and intricate knotting."

Ruby's stomach dropped. She grabbed the case file closest to her and started combing through it. It took a few seconds, but she found what she was looking for. *Strangulation.*

"He didn't hang them," Ruby confirmed. Bellisario nodded.

"What am I missing?" Ruiz looked at Ruby and then at Bellisario.

"Vallejo's seventh victim, Laura Baxter, was hung with a thirteen-threaded rope."

Ruby remembered the case well. Asher had figured out with Julie Hicks, the sixth victim in Vallejo's killing spree, that the number thirteen was a factor in the murders. Vallejo had gone out of his way to make it obvious with Julie. Her car's make and model was 2013, and it had thirteen in the license plate numbers.

They'd gone back and confirmed the other five victims had a connection to the number thirteen too. Laura Baxter was originally listed as a suicide by hanging, something her family heavily disputed. They swore she'd been happy just a few days earlier, that she was making plans to visit friends and family the following month. There was no note, but there also wasn't any evidence anyone else had been in the room when she died.

Asher Carnes was the one who figured it out, like he did with just about everything related to Vallejo. He'd asked for every case file of anyone who'd died in the tri-state area since Brandalyn Kelly's murder. She was the first victim found, but she was actually Vallejo's third victim. He'd beaten her to death. The medical examiner estimated she'd been bludgeoned with a spiked club.

When Asher reviewed her file, he discovered that the medical examiner had stated she'd been hit nine times with something like a bat and then at least four times with brass knuckles. They had left indentions in the wound areas. Later, after Vallejo's arrest, they'd found his cache of weapons, including the brass knuckles and medieval-styled mace he'd used on Brandalyn Kelly.

Thirteen. It didn't take long for Asher to tie a string of deaths to the same perpetrator, some of which weren't initially thought to be homicides.

Ruby learned so much just from watching Asher work. He could see patterns when no one else could. At first, the top brass at the Bureau was skeptical. No one wanted to believe they had a serial killer operating right under their nose, especially not one who could have already had as many as six victims. She remembered being awestruck by Asher's detective work, but also naively hoping he'd gotten it wrong.

Ruby passed the file in her hands to Ruiz and picked up the next one. Before she started to look at the second victim, something clicked. "May I see that file again?"

"Umm. Yeah, sure."

Ruby looked at the name at the top of the file. *Daisy Hauser.*

Hadn't Vallejo said something about daisies? She was sure of it.

Ruby racked her brain, trying to remember his offhand comment, the little bomb he'd planted in her mind just for this moment.

Don't you just look as fresh as a daisy.

Ruby's grip on the file was so tight that her knuckles turned white. He knew the entire time she was sitting there that another one of his psychos were already three kills deep, and she didn't even have a clue. The thought sickened Ruby to the point she thought she might actually vomit. She pulled a piece of spearmint gum out of her pocket, unwrapped it, and stuffed it in her mouth. Hopefully, it would help.

"What is it, Hunter?" Bellisario and Ruiz looked at her like she'd sprouted three heads.

"This is another one of Vallejo's followers."

"There's no way you can tell that by just glancing at the file, Ruby," Ruiz argued. Bellisario stayed silent.

"Yes, I can, and I do. He said something today about daisies. He *knew,* and we only just found her." Ruby looked at the name on the second case file. *Averie Phelps*. She tried to remember every word he'd said, searching for some hint in the dialogue, some notion Vallejo had mentioned the second victim, but nothing stuck out. She'd thought he was just making useless conversation, but she should've known better. Vallejo's words had turned out to be anything *but* useless.

She grabbed the third file from Bellisario's desk and checked the name. *Fran McCormick.* Ruby replayed Vallejo's every word in her memory. Something was there, just on the edge of her recollection.

Are they frantic with worry every time they see your name in the headlines?

Ruby let out a breath she didn't even realize she'd been holding. He was in on it all. "He's toying with us on every one of these cases, giving us just enough to catch up but never enough to get ahead. He didn't just mention daisies today. He also made a comment about people being 'frantic.' As in Fran McCormick."

There was something else, some other clue but she couldn't put her finger on it.

"That's a bit of a stretch, Hunter. The man is in solitary confinement." Gabe's tone contradicted his words. He believed she was onto something, and so did Bellisario. Vallejo was like some sort of serial killer puppet master and only he knew what was going to happen next.

"I am not wrong." Ruby forced the words out through grit teeth. She knew how she sounded. She saw how others at the Bureau looked at her. They all thought she was some kind of Vallejo groupie, that her obsession with the Lucky 13 Killer had exceeded all realms of sanity.

Then it hit her. One of the last comments he made referenced the method of killing.

As much as I'd love to keep you tied up here a little longer, I believe you are due back at the office.

Ruby started to tell Ruiz and Bellisario about the "tied up" comment, but she thought better of it. She already had an uphill battle with trying to prove the other two comments were Vallejo hints. It aggravated her to no end that she was supposedly brought back to the Bureau in the first place *because* of her experience and knowledge of Vincent Vallejo. Now, it seemed like it was *in spite of* it.

Ruiz held his hands up innocently as she fumed. She didn't need or want a partner who didn't believe in her ability to solve a case. Asher always believed in her, always pushed her to look further and really see people. It was one of the things that made him so different than any partner who'd come after him.

Ruby stopped herself. Gabe was not Asher. And he wasn't like anyone else she'd had as a partner since Asher died. None of them had even lasted long enough to solve a case with her.

Ruby and Gabe had solved two cases together, and he was still with her. He hadn't put in a transfer like so many others before him. He'd had her back in the field and saved her more than once. Sure, he gave her a lot of push-back, but then again, she'd done the same with Asher.

Maybe Gabe wasn't the problem she was trying to make him out to be. As Asher would bluntly point out, *she* was the common denominator.

"All right, you two, wheels up in an hour." Bellisario's voice snapped her back to the present.

"Where we headed, boss?"

"The third victim was found in a park area near Akron, Ohio. We'll start with her."

CHAPTER FOUR

"Are you seeing any kind of connection?"

The flight to Akron was approximately ninety minutes, which gave Ruby and Gabe some time to review the case files. Aside from the minor connection Ruby had made to Vallejo from her conversation with him earlier, she could not see another link between the victims.

Ruby shook her head, as if Gabe had read her mind. The three women couldn't be more different.

"There isn't a single thing about these women that overlaps. Not location, not ethnicity, not occupation. *Nothing.*"

The latest one, Daisy Hauser, had been killed in a park, but there was something interesting with that one.

A witness.

Well, a potential witness. The boyfriend, Harrison Cole, had been hit over the head during the murder and was now in the ICU in a medically induced coma.

So, essentially, nothing helpful.

She watched Ruiz read through each case. He spread the three files out in front of him and rubbed his face. He looked about as frustrated as she felt. Ruby wondered how long it would be before Gabe had had enough of the morgues, crime scene tape, and murder boards. She was honestly surprised he hadn't already left. Ruby doubted anyone in the office pool had bet on him lasting as her partner this long.

Gabe Ruiz was very different from any other partners she'd had, including Asher. He was athletic and former military, although he hadn't told her much about either. She didn't mind the mystery. It was better not to know. No attachments. After Asher, she couldn't risk getting to know anyone Vallejo or some other sicko might target.

Ruby could tell Gabe was all about the chase. He got a thrill out of kicking in doors and running down bad guys. He'd gotten to do that a couple times recently, but that wasn't typical. Their job was more *cerebral* than physical. Most of the time, anyway. She was curious what kind of experience he'd had at the Oregon field office.

Oregon had its share of serial killers over the years. Ruby had studied a few at the Academy, not that anything in those books had ever prepared her for Vincent Vallejo. She remembered something Asher had said to her in those last days.

Some places are hunting grounds and some places are breeding grounds, but rarely are they both.

Based on what Ruby knew, Oregon was more a hunting ground for the Vallejos of the world. That could mean Gabe Ruiz had been either very busy or very bored. She figured by his continued discomfort in these cases it was more of the latter.

I get to watch women drop like flies while we count things in an office.

Ruby recalled Gabe's words as if he'd just said them to her. His tone had been a mix of disbelief and frustration. She understood his perspective, though, more than she wanted to admit. Since Vallejo's arrest, she saw murder everywhere.

The sickness, it spreads.

Her mother's words were always at the edge of her psyche, falling into her consciousness more than she wanted. Maybe because they were true. While Carole Hunter had no formal education, she could see people for what they really were. It was one of the reasons Ruby's relationship with her mother was always such a challenge. She constantly felt like a disappointment, like she had never been good enough or made the right choices.

Ruby wasn't much of a fan of being in the field. She could hold her own, but she preferred the mental gymnastics to running down perps. As Asher always said, this job wasn't for everyone. Maybe it wasn't the right place for Gabe, but Ruby hadn't seen enough to know for sure.

"Do you want to talk me through the victimology?" Ruby asked, extending the smallest olive branch his way.

Ruby had never been good at sharing. She was an only child, and it showed. Asher was the first person who showed her how fun it could be, how rewarding, to share her life with someone.

She still remembered the first time Asher divvied up the food they'd ordered as if it was for both of them. Ruby was infuriated. She'd ordered the fried chicken wings, her favorite, and he'd ordered dumplings. When the food arrived, he took half of her wings and gave her half of the dumplings. She'd never had dumplings before, so she didn't even know if she liked them.

"How are you ever going to know if you like something if you don't try it?" he'd asked her innocently, as if he hadn't just turned her world upside down.

"I ordered the chicken wings because they're my favorite, and I *wanted* chicken wings. *All* of them," she'd complained.

"I'm sorry. I'll give you them if you want them. But first, try the dumplings. You'll like them."

He was right, as always, and that only pissed her off even more. The angrier she got at the ridiculous situation, the more amusing Asher seemed to find in it. That was the first time she really shared a meal with someone and also the first night she stayed over.

Ruby's gesture to talk through the case with Gabe Ruiz might not have seemed like much, but it was a big step for her. She still didn't know him all that well, and she wasn't sure how much she trusted him.

"Yeah, sure," Gabe said as he sifted back through the files and pulled one out of the pile.

Ruby pulled out her notepad and prepared to make any pertinent notes based on their conversation.

"The first victim, Fran McCormick, was married, twenty-six years old, and had short, black hair. Hazel eyes. She was average sized I'd say, and according to her license, just above five feet tall. Two children, both under five. And … she worked at a bank."

Ruby looked at Fran's DMV picture. Fran McCormick had a pretty smile and weary eyes, like any twenty-something mom with two toddlers, a husband, and a job. Fran could have been her neighbor, or someone she'd passed in the produce section at the grocery store. Ruby realized the only thing about the woman that stood out was that her name wasn't short for something like Francis.

She studied one of the crime scene photos. Fran McCormick's face was unrecognizable. The brutality of the strangulation was clear from the heavy bruising and petechiae. There were scratch marks around the rope, making it clear that Fran McCormick didn't go quietly.

Gabe set one file down and picked up another.

"Averie Phelps, the second victim, was divorced, thirty-five years old, and had long, curly, red hair and blue eyes. Her license says she was five-five and 200 pounds. It says here she's got a sixteen-year-old son who lives with her ex. She was a realtor, but it doesn't look like she'd been actively working for several months."

Gabe handed Ruby Averie's picture. Her DMV photo was recent, and she wasn't smiling. Averie Phelps just looked straight ahead, almost like it was a mug shot.

"Nasty divorce?"

"Yeah. The ex-husband got the house too."

Ruby nodded. She glanced at one of Averie Phelps's crime scene photos long enough to confirm it looked almost exactly like Fran McCormick's. Then she handed it back to Gabe along with the DMV photo.

"Daisy Hauser, our most recent victim, was a nineteen-year-old college student with shoulder-length, chestnut brown hair, and brown eyes. No children. She worked part-time at the college library as part of the work study program."

Ruby couldn't stomach to look at any more dead women.

"Is this how things were with … Vallejo?"

She noticed Ruiz always hesitated just a little before saying Vallejo's name. Most people did, except Ruby. She refused to let anyone else see how much fear he inspired in her. At that moment, she realized Vincent Vallejo was not just her bogeyman anymore.

She nodded. "It was a long twenty-four months."

Gabe shook his head in disbelief. She'd seen that look before. Too many times to count. It was the same look on every one of her previous partners' faces shortly before they put in a transfer. They hadn't signed on for all the baggage Ruby had to carry.

She thought about her previous partners and what she wished she'd done differently with them. Two things stood out. Assertiveness and Transparency, both of which she'd struggled with since she was a kid.

Secrets make you sick, Ruby. Just like the people you chase.

Her mother's opinions rolled around her mind like bowling balls, smashing her confidence and sense of self upon every impact. Ruby's mother had never hesitated to share her judgmental perspective on Ruby's life. She'd never understood why Ruby would want to be in law enforcement, constantly putting her life in danger. She also didn't approve. Neither of her parents did.

After Asher's death, Ruby had made the mistake of visiting her parents. She remembered thinking that was what she was supposed to do. Her heart was broken, her life shattered. That's what Asher would've done. He'd even said to her on more than one occasion, "Home heals the hurt." He'd obviously never met her parents, and she'd never gotten the chance to really tell him much about them.

Her home was never going to be a place of healing. It never had been, and she knew based on her most recent visit that it wasn't going to change. Neither was the Bureau as long as Vallejo was sending new killers her way every time she turned around.

Ruby needed a partner who was willing to stick by her through the tough cases, take risks, and trust she knew what she was talking about. Especially when it came to Vallejo. She wanted to believe Gabe could be in it for the long haul, but if he wasn't, she didn't want to be blindsided.

"Hey, can you do me a favor, Ruiz?"

"Sure, what do you need?"

"It's actually two favors, I guess. First, I really don't want to have to break-in another partner mid-case. It creates too much drama, and it's bad for the case. Second, please have the decency to tell me before you put in the paperwork. Okay?"

Gabe just stared at her. She didn't know him well enough to know what he was thinking, but she was pretty sure it was nothing good. Ruby felt her wall of fake confidence crumble a little. *Maybe she was wrong about him.*

"We're partners, Hunter. Until you say otherwise."

Ruby didn't know what to say. His tone was so matter of fact, there was no room for argument. She half-nodded, half-shrugged. Gabe shifted his focus back to the files in front of him. She could tell from his hunched shoulders, glowering look, and clenched jaw that he likely wasn't going to say another word the rest of the flight. Ruby wasn't sure what to make of it.

The next thing Ruby heard was the pilot's voice welcoming them to their destination.

As they touched down, Ruby checked her phone. She had three missed calls and a voicemail from Executive Assistant Director Barrett Murphy. *I'll listen to it later,* she thought, putting her phone away. There was nothing Murphy was going to say to help her on this case, and whatever he did have to talk to her about could wait.

CHAPTER FIVE

He was touching where the hands of God once were. The thought washed over him like holy water.

The man gently held the envelope up to the light to inspect its contents before he opened it. His hands trembled with anticipation. He put the letter down for a moment and wiped his hands off on his trousers. A light film of sweat coated his palms, the excitement almost too much to contain.

Once he was confident his hands were dry, he traced the indented script of his name and address across the front.

He sat down at his large, oak desk and placed the letter in front of him. He wanted this moment to last forever. He could not even imagine what the letter said. He knew his limits, and whatever was written was sacred and beyond anything the man could have thought of.

The man opened the righthand drawer and withdrew the solid sterling, silver letter opener. He read the personalized inscription across the blade. *Per lunam ad astra.* He'd had it for almost a decade, his most treasured item. The words meant, "Through the moon to the stars," and they were just for him.

The letter opener previously belonged to his Psychology of Religion professor. He remembered the first time he'd ever seen it. The man had stayed after class to talk with the professor. It was the last day he could withdraw from the term without failing or being on the hook financially for the whole semester. What had started out as innocent frat parties and weekend fun had become something darker and more sinister.

The man couldn't remember the last time he'd slept in his own bed, but he always remembered to show up for this class. He loved the Psychology of Religion class, and he had been doing well in it. He was failing everything else, but this class kept his attention. He always felt like the professor understood him, spoke straight to him. So, the man felt like he should at least say goodbye before dropping the class. It seemed like the right thing to do. He wasn't sure why at the time, but now hc understood it was all part of a much bigger plan.

The professor was opening his mail as the rest of the class filed out. He'd watched the professor smoothly slice open each letter, each stroke a cut to his confidence. The man hesitated and then decided he should probably just leave. It's not like anyone would notice he wasn't there anymore.

Then the professor had called out to him. He said *his name*. The man didn't think *anyone* knew who he was.

He had hung his head as he approached the professor, filled with shame and humiliation. He told the professor how much he loved the class, but due to unforeseen circumstances he was having to withdraw. He apologized and assured the professor the class was one of the best he'd ever taken.

The professor had listened intently as the man spoke, never interrupting, taking it all in. Then the professor asked, "How can I help?"

The professor was so genuine with his query, like he really wanted to help the man any way he could. They were just four simple words, but together they were the first time since he was a child that someone had expressed any interest in him.

Overwhelmed by such a simple gesture of concern, the man had first been reluctant to speak. But his professor had a way of drawing people out. Eventually, he explained his predicament, how he owed all the wrong people money he didn't have. The man admitted for the first time that he was a slave to his demons and the vices he'd picked up along the way. He knew there wasn't much left in this life for him, but he was hoping stepping back would give him the chance to get himself straight.

The professor had looked at him with warmth and understanding. There was no judgment. No pity. Only kindness and compassion. The man hadn't known much of either in his life, and the professor gave it so freely that it had made him weep.

Before that moment, the man hadn't wanted to admit his life was out of control. He didn't want to believe he had a problem. With booze. Pills. Women. Staying up until dawn with no one he knew and waking up in beds that weren't his own. He was living the college life. That's all. Or at least that's what he'd been trying to tell himself every day for over a month.

But the professor knew better. He knew the people the man had gotten mixed up with, what kind of danger he was in. He also knew if the man left school, he'd likely never come back, and that was not a solution the professor was willing to accept.

The professor had told the man to sit in the front row while he made two phone calls. He walked over to his desk, picked up his phone, and walked out of the classroom. The man was confused. He wasn't sure if he should stay put or leave. Just when he was about to get up, the professor walked back into the room.

Then the professor had sat down next to him. The man didn't understand what was going on or why someone like the professor even cared. He was just some punk, nineteen-year-old junkie to everyone else.

"You're going to come stay with me for a little while, and you're not withdrawing from school. Understand?"

The man hadn't known what to say. Why would this man help him? How? He didn't understand. The professor assured him everything was above board and not to worry.

The professor had explained that he'd acquired his drug debt. Somehow, he knew just who his dealers were and just how to find them. So now instead of owing people who were ready to break his kneecaps, he owed the professor. The professor also said that the only way the man was going to pay back his debt was by getting clean and getting an education. The professor was happy to help him do both, but the man had to be serious about it and make some real changes.

It was astonishing, the humanity this person had shown him in a matter of just a few minutes. The man hadn't had anyone in his life for almost a year, no one he could turn to for help. Yet here was this relative stranger stepping up to help him like they'd known each other forever. The thought of what the professor had done for him still brought tears to his eyes. No one had ever reached out to him or been willing to believe in him the way the professor had.

It took a few minutes for the man to comprehend what the professor was telling him. Partly because he couldn't believe anyone would want to help someone like him, and partly because it was an absolute miracle—something the man had never put a lot of faith in.

The professor then asked a question the man would never forget.

"Don't you know how special you are?" The man could not think of a worthy response, so he just shook his head. The professor nodded with a knowing look. "The stars still shine even with the brightest and fullest of moons in their midst. And you, my dear friend, are made of the stuff of stars. I see how brightly you shine even when you can't. And by the time I'm done with you, everyone will see it too."

The man was stunned by the professor's declaration. He saw something in the man that seemed impossible. The man had never thought of himself as anyone special. He was just a regular guy who had made a lot of bad decisions. But not to the professor. He was something more, a protégé in the making.

The man sobered up with the professor's help and ended the semester successfully. For the first time in his life, he was proud of himself. The professor was too. At ninety days sober, the professor gave the man a gift. He opened it to find what he thought was a replica of the professor's letter opener. The professor assured him it was not a copy.

"Someone gave this to me after I'd been through a challenging time, much like what you've just been through, and the words inscribed have helped me stay the course. I hope it will do the same for you."

The letter opener was so much more than a simple reminder. It was his connection to a titan of a man who'd reached out to him in the abyss he'd made of his life and pulled him to safety. It was the unspoken promise the man had made to the professor and to himself, a promise he was finally able to fulfill.

With trembling hands, the man slipped the blade into the corner of the envelope and, in one easy motion, cut it open. He carefully removed the letter, unfolded it, and laid it out flat before him.

The man read each word several times, tracing the handwriting as if it were written by God himself. In a way, it was. The man who'd written it was a god, not only to him, but also to so many others. He saw them for who they really were, who they could be. He'd saved them when the rest of the world turned its back on them, and he believed in each and every one of them. They all had their own promises to keep, their own destinies to achieve.

The man pulled out two laminating sheets from the lefthand drawer and sealed the letter between them. It was something he wanted to keep forever, so he had to preserve it like the others. As he returned the letter opener to the righthand drawer, he noticed his desk calendar. Joy filled every crevice of his being. There were only a few more days until the next full moon.

He looked back over the letter once more and read the last line over and over again.

No one will ever shine brighter than you, not even the brightest and fullest of stars.

CHAPTER SIX

Not only was the hike to Orion's Lookout trickier than Ruby had anticipated, but the rains that had passed had likely wiped clean the crime scene. It was slippery with mud and lined with slick tree roots primed for tripping. She was grateful she'd worn her nonslip shoes, although they were probably the ugliest in her closet.

Gabe had no trouble with the steep route. Ruby wasn't surprised. He'd never admitted he liked hiking, but she was sure he did. She'd let him pass her while she kept a watchful eye on every step. He was confident in his footing, moving through the trees like it was his natural habitat.

Ruby caught up to Gabe as the trail opened to a large, circular meadow surrounded by trees. Orion's Lookout was beautiful if you liked that sort of thing. Ruby didn't. She liked the city lights, car horns, and every single thing that reminded her she wasn't that little girl living in the run-down trailer park anymore.

"Not sure what you're expecting to find out here, but feel free to look around." The local deputy made it clear from the moment he picked them up at the airport that they were too late. Though the case had just come across the FBI's desk recently, it'd been three weeks since the crime scene had been processed. There wasn't anything for them to find. Ruby didn't care if it was an inconvenience or didn't make sense. She insisted they see where Daisy Hauser's life had ended.

Gabe walked off to the left with his camera while she evaluated the area. He liked to document what they saw whether it was through pictures or extensive notes. It was one thing about him she'd come to truly appreciate. He took his job seriously, which was not always the case with her previous partners.

They had just come from the parking lot, so this was likely the main entrance. Ruby looked around, but she wasn't able to discern if there was any more trails into the meadow.

"Is there another way to get here besides the way we just came?" she called out to the deputy.

"Yeah, down at the other end, but it's got a lot of overgrowth, so it probably hasn't been used in a while."

The deputy motioned toward the right corner at the far end of the meadow. Of course, it was at the other end. Ruby slowly made her way across the space, traversing through the muck. It had apparently rained recently, leaving the ground soggy and difficult to navigate. She had never wished more for a pair of rain boots.

As she reached the far side of Orion's Lookout, Ruby wondered if this was where the killer had lain in wait. It was the perfect spot to hide with all the tall, brush grass and saplings. Given that the murder took place late at night, there was no way Daisy could've seen the killer in the dark until it was too late.

"Find anything?"

Ruby jumped at the sound of Gabe's voice breaking into her thoughts. She started to scold him for sneaking up on her, but then she caught the tail end of a smile swiping across his face. Maybe he wasn't as mad at her about the whole transfer conversation as she'd thought. Ruby's anxiety went into overdrive any time she thought she'd said or done something wrong. It was the product of growing up in an unstable house filled with unending conflict.

Fighting a war on two fronts is more likely to lead to death than peace. Asher had told her that the first day she was assigned to him. He was always saying things like that, but she knew what he meant. Partners with problems didn't solve cases.

Ruby hadn't liked Asher Carnes when she was first assigned to him. He seemed arrogant and like too much of a know-it-all. She'd been jealous of her fellow Academy graduates who were paired with partners more their own age and experience level. She'd been too stupid to know any better.

The abrupt sound of a twig snapping nearby refocused Ruby's attention.

"No, but based on where the body was positioned, she was headed that way. I was thinking maybe he'd hid himself in the brush, but it doesn't look like anything's been over here in a while."

Gabe nodded, but he still snapped a couple of photos. "Wish that boyfriend wasn't in a coma. Bet he could tell us a few things."

She nodded absently.

"I think I've gotten photos from every angle. Was there anything else you wanted me to get a shot of?"

Ruby shook her head, and they started back to the other side.

"It's dryer on that side. Probably because of the rocks. The deputy said they found a wicker basket and a blanket on that large, flat rock. We could take a quick look if you want."

Ruby's eyes followed to where Gabe was pointing. There was a rock formation with several different sizes and shapes of rocks. Ruby looked back at the overgrown brush and then forward to where the trailhead was. Daisy Hauser was running toward the parking lot, so it was feasible the killer had come from this direction.

Ruby looked over at the rocky area once more. She noticed there was one rock larger and flatter than the others. It was the perfect size for a picnic for two.

"Do you recall what the file said about time of death?"

"It was sometime after midnight."

"Kind of late for a picnic, don't you think?"

"Well, the deputy did say this is kind of a popular make-out spot."

Something clicked in Ruby's head. She looked up. "It's also probably a great spot to see the stars."

Gabe looked up for just a moment and then looked back at her. He sucked in a long, deep breath before sighing loudly. "Is this another Vallejo thing?"

"Possibly."

Gabe shook his head and rolled his eyes, not wanting to believe Vallejo was connected to every murder they encountered.

For what it was worth, Ruby didn't want there to be another connection between Vallejo and this case. Or any of her cases for that matter. She wanted to be done with him, for him to wither away into dust behind the walls of Boone Correctional Facility. But she also knew from his word games that this killer was likely one of his disciples, doing his bidding where he couldn't.

Gabe glanced at his watch. "Was there anything else you wanted to see here?"

"No, let's go see the medical examiner."

CHAPTER SEVEN

The ride to the medical examiner's office took forty-five minutes. Ruby used the time to look up more information about Orion's Lookout and Parkville, the surrounding town. The area was more of a suburb of Akron than its own town. However, there was a main street with a local grocery store and pharmacy on one side of the street, and the fire department and police station were on the other side.

Ruby had seen a lot of towns like Parkville in the last few years. They had little variations here and there, like a movie theater or an arcade, but mostly they were the same, just with different names.

Vallejo preferred small towns. His kills had more impact there. They reached more people and devastated more lives.

His eighth victim was found in a town much like Parkville. Naomi Jones's murder had been the biggest headline in Earnest, Virginia, since it had become a township. Everyone knew Naomi or her family. But her death was what everyone remembered the most, which was Vallejo's point.

Naomi Jones disappeared on November 30th, her twenty-second birthday. Her family had planned a surprised party for her, but she never came home. Her car was still at work, but she was nowhere to be found.

Vallejo had snatched her in broad daylight as she'd walked to her car to go home. No one saw a thing. No one even thought something bad had happened. Earnest, Virginia, was not a place where people were kidnapped, much less murdered. Vallejo changed that forever.

He locked Naomi Jones in a dark, damp basement with no heat for nineteen days. He left her four gallons of Pedialyte and two boxes of saltines. It was enough to keep her alive but that was about it.

Then, just as the clock hit midnight on December 18th, Vallejo released thirteen timberland rattlesnakes into the basement and left her to die. By that point, she was hypothermic from the freezing temperatures and couldn't have escaped the snakes even if she had wanted to. The young woman's death was so gruesome that her parents had the body cremated and opted for a memorial service to say their goodbyes.

The town was devastated by her death. The violence and cruelty Vallejo had inflicted on Naomi Jones sent residents packing and kept tourists away for over a year. Businesses closed and soon Earnest, Virginia, wasn't much of a town anymore. Vincent Vallejo hadn't just destroyed Naomi's life and the lives of her family. He'd taken everything from the town that loved her.

It took Ruby and Asher weeks before they realized Vallejo had taken Naomi Jones at the beginning of the thirteenth astrological sign's cycle, and he'd killed her on its last day. Ophiuchus wasn't commonly recognized as part of the astrological calendar, but when it was included, it changed all the dates of the other signs.

Vincent Vallejo had planned out every murder in painstaking detail. He knew Naomi Jones's birthday, about the surprise party, and exactly where she would be for him to grab her. Asher initially assumed Vallejo learned all he needed to know about Naomi through social media and surveillance. Except Naomi didn't have any social media. She'd had no online footprint whatsoever.

Ruby combed through every statement they had from her family and friends to try and figure out what they were missing. She remembered one of Naomi's sisters had made an odd comment like "this was the longest she'd ever stayed at a job before." Once Ruby figured out which sister had said it, she called her to find out more.

It turned out that Naomi was a victim of stalking her junior year in high school. A stranger she'd smiled at in the grocery store fixated on her for thirteen months, showing up everywhere Naomi went. He'd called and hung up several times a day, and he left notes on her car, in her locker, and at her after school job. The local police thought it was innocent, nothing to worry about. They monitored her home phone and drove by her house randomly, but none of them believed it was anything serious.

Naomi recorded every incident in her journal and what, if anything, the police had done about it. In one entry, she'd written how her stalker seemed to know things about her she had never told anyone. She shared how terrified she was of snakes, something she hadn't told anyone, but her stalker, a perfect stranger, knew.

After a couple of weeks of silence, Naomi thought maybe the stalker had finally given up. Maybe it *was* something innocuous, and she was being paranoid. Then when she went to get in her car before school, she saw a timberland rattlesnake in the passenger seat of her Ford Focus.

Naomi immediately called the police, who told her finding a snake in her car wasn't that uncommon this time of year. They suggested she call pest control and all but told her that they thought she was being overly dramatic. The officer on the phone had even gone so far as to suggest she was making a big deal out of nothing, which was costing time and money as well as taking resources away from *real* crimes being solved.

A couple of days later, Naomi's stalker broke into her home, hoping to do God knows what, but she wasn't there. He smashed every photo her parents had of her in the house and set her bed on fire. The police finally took notice, but the man was never caught.

Since then, the only thing Naomi was consistent about was how often she changed her routines. She never kept a job longer than ninety days. She changed her locks regularly. She moved every six months. She'd done everything possible to keep herself safe for fear that her stalker might return to finish what he'd started.

But Vallejo knew. Even though her files were sealed because she'd been underage. Even though Naomi lived by the strictest code and had taken extreme measures to protect herself. He knew things about her he shouldn't have.

He knows things about me. Things I have never told anyone.

Ruby would never forget Asher's words and how he sounded when he said them to her. It was the first time she had ever heard real fear in his voice. Now, she realized he'd been trying to warn her.

Vallejo wasn't like any other killer Asher Carnes had seen, and that was saying something. He'd been the most experienced agent in their office, with more than a dozen solved cases including three serial killers. But Vincent Vallejo scared him.

Ruby still didn't understand why Asher had decided on that last night to follow up on a tip without her. It was the one thing he'd told her not to do from the first time they'd met. And it was the reason he was dead. He had no backup, and no one to help him.

She knew if Asher were still alive that he'd tell her it didn't matter, that there was nothing she could've done. Hell, she likely would've gotten them both killed. But she couldn't shake the feeling it was somehow her fault or that she could've done something to save him.

Ruby played the "what if" game far too often when it came to Asher's death. In the end, it didn't matter. Asher was still dead, and Ruby was still trying to stop Vallejo.

Ruby heard Gabe's voice and looked up.

"Ruby?"

"Sorry, what was that?"

"Did you find anything?"

"Vallejo's eighth victim had an astrology connection. She was born on the first day of Ophiuchus, the thirteenth astrological sign, and killed on the last day of it. Did you see anything along those lines in the file?"

"Nothing that stood out. Is Orion related to astrology? Maybe that's the connection."

"I am not aware of any zodiac sign associated with Orion, but maybe it's more of an *astronomical* connection than an astrological one. May I see the other two files please?"

Gabe pulled the files out and handed them to her. She looked up the town in Virginia where Fran McCormick was killed. Then she looked up the city where Averie Phelps died. Ruby was trying to figure out what kind of configuration the three points on a map would make. She stared at the lines for a second.

"It looks like a greater-than sign," Gabe said, holding up his right hand like an open mouth. Ruby frowned. "What?"

"There aren't any astrological signs or constellations that look like a greater-than sign."

"So? What's your point?"

"Every constellation that has this kind of shape in it has a lot more than three points. Which means, we're possibly looking at a lot more victims. There may already be a lot more victims we just haven't connected to this guy yet. Just like Vallejo," Ruby explained.

"Let's not get ahead of ourselves just yet and break out the 'Six Degrees of Vallejo' game. You're also assuming your astrological angle is the right one."

Gabe had a point. Was she trying to fit squares inside circles, or was she looking at triangles and seeing the potential for squares?

This is what Vallejo did. He lured her in and dangled just enough clues to send her down the wrong path. Then he'd strike when he was sure she was looking the other way. Vallejo's two disciples had done the same thing. Brett Thorne, Elias Delko, Kenny Barton, Miles Barker. They were all just distractions so the killers could continue their work. She wasn't sure yet if this killer would try the same pattern, but she had to keep an open mind. Otherwise, she'd just fall right back into his trap.

Ruby understood she was racing against a clock, but she had no idea how much time she had left. She didn't want to take the chance of going down the wrong path again and wasting the opportunity to find this killer before he struck again. They *had* to figure out how he was picking his victims, what the pattern was. Before it was too late.

CHAPTER EIGHT

"Based on the angle of the rope, the perpetrator is significantly larger than these women. All of them are five-foot-eight or shorter. He's at least six-foot-three, if not taller. He's also adept with his hands. The rope is handmade down to every last strand, and the three pieces we have were cut from a longer piece."

The morgue looked exactly like every other morgue Ruby had been in since starting at the FBI. Same pale blue tones on the walls and tile floors. This one was smaller, but otherwise there were no variations from anything she'd seen before. None of these places ever looked any different.

Ruby listened as the ME explained the wound similarities on each victim. Daisy Hauser's body was in front of them, but the bodies of Fran McCormick and Averie Phelps were being shared live on two monitors by the MEs in their towns. Given the distance, it was the only way to see bodies from three different states at the same time.

"Do you have the victim's belongings?" Gabe asked.

"Yes, follow me."

Ruby and Gabe followed the ME out of the morgue and into a makeshift storage room. There were two industrial, metal shelves filled with file boxes, each marked with a case number in black marker. There was also a stainless-steel worktable, much like the one Daisy Hauser's body rested on in the other room.

The room looked older, with cracks near the ceiling from the building settling. Ruby realized the other room was likely a new addition. She highly doubted Parkville had enough death to deal with that they needed to expand the morgue four more feet.

The ME pulled a box from the shelves and set it on the table. "Let me know if you need anything else." A moment later, Ruby and Gabe were alone.

Gabe pulled the top of the box off and set it down on the table. The evidence in the box was bagged and tagged, so they didn't have to worry about contaminating it with fingerprints.

"Look at this."

Ruby pulled one of the bags out of the box. In it, there was a pack of tarot cards with a red rubber band around them. The edges of the cards were well-worn, and the pale pink color on the back of the cards was faded as if they had been handled a lot. The Lovers card was on top. Two people in ornate Venetian masks passionately embraced each other under a glowing full moon. The vibrant colors were highlighted with gold foil as if the heavens were shining down on the couple.

"Maybe the astrology connection wasn't that farfetched after all."

Gabe shrugged as he went through a couple of other bags. He held one up to Ruby. It was a business card for The Mystic Spirit, some sort of metaphysical, New Age spiritual shop.

"'Crystals, candles, and readings to awaken your true potential.' What does that even mean?"

Ruby chuckled at Gabe's confusion. "They don't have tarot card readers in Oregon?"

"I'm sure they do. I've just never been to one. Have you?"

"Maybe once or twice when I was younger. Who knows ... I might even have a tarot card deck of my own," Ruby teased.

"Okay, but what's the point of that hocus pocus crap?"

She had to laugh at that. Her previous readings had promised riches and fame. They never would've predicted the life she had now. "I have no idea, but I think we should go check it out. Maybe someone there will remember our victim."

CHAPTER NINE

The Mystic Spirit was one of several stores in a strip mall on the edge of town. A neon purple welcome sign blinked on the glass door, but something was off with its rhythm, like it was slowly dying. Life-size posters of tarot cards hung in each window, one was the Wheel of Fortune and the other was The Lovers. It looked exactly like the one in Daisy's tarot deck.

"Do you think she got her cards from here?" Ruby asked as she nodded toward the poster.

"Possibly. The deck looked pretty worn, though. This place doesn't seem that old."

Ruby pushed the door open and heard a bell chime. She looked up and noticed a brass bell hanging directly above them as they entered. A sweet, musky scent overwhelmed Ruby's senses, giving her an instant headache.

"You okay?"

"Yeah, I am just not a fan of strong perfumes and stuff." Ruby opened the door to get some fresh air. Just as she did, a short, plump woman draped in dark purple iridescent robes and a large, purple amulet appeared.

"Welcome, welcome to The Mystic Spirit. I am your guide, Madame Lunetta."

The woman had long, black, curly hair that looked like a wig from a Walmart Halloween costume and elaborate eye makeup with lots of glitter and false lashes. She looked like she was in her late fifties, but it was hard to tell with everything plastered on her face the way it was. Her nails were longer than Ruby thought they would be for a tarot card reader and painted a bright fuchsia. Ruby couldn't quite place the woman's accent, only that it wasn't American.

Ruby and Gabe identified themselves with their badges.

"Do you have somewhere we can speak privately, Madame Lunetta?"

"Of course, and please call me Debra Jean. Madame Lunetta is my stage name."

Debra Jean's accent shifted from some non-descript European origin to distinctly midwestern. Ruby caught Gabe's look of surprise and smirked. "So, you're not a real psychic?"

"Oh, no, I am. But people don't seem interested in taking advice about their future from a small-town hick named Debra Jean."

Ruby and Gabe followed the woman into a back room where all the walls were draped with the same dark purple fabric as her robes. A round table sat in the middle of the room with a sturdy, wooden chair on the right and two lavender armchairs on the left. A black tapestry with the phases of the moon in a circle covered the table, and a deck of tarot cards sat off to the right. Behind the wooden chair, there was a large bookcase filled with books, candles, and crystals. Ruby wondered if Debra Jean sold all the items in the room in her store, or if some things were just for show.

"Please have a seat."

Gabe and Ruby took their seats, but Debra Jean remained standing with her hands clasped in front of her. Ruby glanced at Gabe, unsure if she was exerting some strange need for control or what. He didn't look too sure himself.

Ruby wondered if they should insist she sit, but she didn't say anything. She watched Gabe reach into the satchel where he had the files of the three victims. He pulled out an enlarged photo of Daisy's DMV picture.

"Madame ... Sorry, Debra Jean, can you please tell me if you've seen this woman?"

Ruby watched Debra Jean shift her weight from one foot to the other. Her eyes seemed to look everywhere but at the photo. She hesitated too long, and Ruby suspected she was trying to figure out if she should lie to them or not.

"This is Daisy Hauser. You may have seen her on the news, but we have reason to believe she was in your shop at least once in the last couple of months. Please take a look."

Ruby took the photo from Gabe and handed it to Debra Jean. The woman made a sound like she was sucking her teeth before sighing loudly. She looked at the bookshelf behind her and fiddled with a couple of items before pulling out an eyeglass case. She slipped on the readers and set the case on the table.

"Hmmm. I am not sure. Maybe. Most of my customers are young women just like her."

Ruby could not help but notice how fidgety Debra Jean was. She wondered why the woman insisted on standing. Was she trying to maintain a position or power or was she hiding something?

"She had a deck of tarot cards that look just like the ones on your window."

Ruby gave Gabe a pointed look. He was always so quick to interrogate. Sometimes cutting to the chase meant cutting out potentially important information. Eagerness did not solve cases.

"Ahhh, yes. I remember now. She was very sweet and thought she might be in love. She wanted to know if he was 'the one.' I believe I remember talking with her about her future, how bright and beautiful it was going to be."

"She was murdered over three weeks ago."

This time, Ruby didn't mind Gabe's cut-and-dry approach. She could see the wheels turning in Debra Jean's mind. Something was not quite right, but Ruby could not pinpoint what it was.

"Oh yes, yes, yes. That's right. After she left, I had a terrible premonition something bad was going to happen to her. I tried to contact her, but I didn't have her number. Usually, my clients sign up for the Mystic Membership so they can get a discount on future readings. She didn't, and that was the first and only time she had come in my shop."

Debra Jean continued to shift her weight, and Ruby realized she *wanted* to sit down but for some reason wouldn't.

"Ma'am, could you please take a seat. This is important."

Ruby's sharp tone caught Debra Jean's attention, and she did as she was told. As she lowered herself into the chair across from them, Ruby identified why the woman had insisted on standing for so long. Debra Jean had been trying to hide something.

Situated between two books and angled right at Ruby and Gabe was a small video camera. It was designed to be overlooked, blend in, and was very expensive. Ruby knew professional surveillance equipment when she saw it.

"Debra Jean, do you record your readings?"

The woman's eyes widened. "Absolutely not. This is a legitimate business, and I have a stellar reputation in the community."

Gabe jumped in, and Ruby knew he'd seen the camera too. "Then you won't mind us calling the judge for a warrant, right?"

"A warrant for what?"

"To search the premises. You see, Daisy Hauser is connected to some other open cases and, right now, you're our only lead. Based on that alone, I imagine we'll have the paperwork approved and in hand within probably half an hour."

Gabe stood up and pulled out his phone.

The woman's eyes went wide. "Wait! What are you doing?"

"As you said, Debra Jean, this is a legitimate business, right? I'm calling a judge."

Ruby looked over at him, impressed. They both knew they didn't have enough for a warrant, but Debra Jean didn't. Gabe's poker face was far better than she'd anticipated, and Debra Jean was terrified.

"Okay, okay. Yes, I record *some* of my sessions. It helps me connect to the spirits so I can be more in tune with my clients' needs, especially if they have complex concerns."

Ruby folded her arms. Debra Jean was an absolute fraud just as she'd suspected.

"We're going to need to see the video of your reading with Daisy."

Debra Jean nodded and scurried out of the room. Ruby looked at Gabe. He rolled his eyes and shook his head.

"It's amazing the people we get to meet in this business," Gabe sighed as he relaxed into the chair next to her.

"No kidding."

Debra Jean reappeared approximately two minutes later with a laptop. She placed it on the table in front of Ruby and Gabe.

"Just hit enter to play the video. The session was twenty-five minutes."

Ruby tapped the key and immediately a vibrant Daisy Hauser came to life on the screen. Gabe leaned in, watching just as intently.

In the video, Daisy was animated as she talked about her new boyfriend, Harrison. She was bright-eyed with pink cheeks like she'd just come in from the wintery outdoors. She seemed light and happy, like she really was in love. Ruby remembered what that felt like, along with the pain of its absence.

Ruby noticed Daisy did most of the talking, with Debra Jean only nodding and reassuring her to continue. Daisy's voice was lyrical, even when she gushed with excitement over her relationship. So much life in one person.

While this killer didn't seem to have a type, Vallejo did, and Daisy Hauser fit it to a "T." Asher had thought maybe he'd coveted the vibrancy of someone like Daisy, or maybe he'd been hurt by a woman like that in his past. Ruby didn't think either theory was accurate. Vallejo just seemed like a man who wanted to cut down life everywhere he saw it.

Halfway through the video, Daisy mentioned one of her neighbors always lurking around. She said she was scared of him, worried he might do something. She asked Madame Lunetta if he was going to hurt her. Debra Jean pet the young woman's hand like she was a dog and smiled.

"You have a bright and beautiful future ahead of you, Daisy. Don't worry about that creep." Debra Jean was in full Madame Lunetta mode, accent and all. Daisy sighed and nodded in agreement.

"When was this session?" Gabe asked as they watched Daisy walk off camera.

"Let me look at my session log. Just a moment."

Debra Jean pulled a thin ledger from her bookshelf and skimmed the pages for Daisy's entry.

"Here it is. Four weeks ago, to the day."

Gabe looked at Ruby. Could this be the break in the case they needed to catch this guy? Ruby certainly hoped so.

"We're going to need a copy of this video before we go."

Debra Jean handed over a thumb drive as if she already knew they were going to ask her for it.

"What about the search warrant?"

"As long as you continue to cooperate, Debra Jean, I think we can put a pause on any legal paperwork for now."

Gabe looked the woman straight in the eyes as he issued the warning. Debra Jean quickly nodded, seemingly to answer any and all questions.

He gave her a nod in return and then walked toward the front of the store.

Ruby hesitated. "You know, we're not supposed to have all the answers."

"Maybe, but it doesn't stop anyone from looking. Including you." The woman smiled knowingly at Ruby.

She wasn't sure what to make of the comment, nor did she want to find out. "Goodbye, Debra Jean."

Ruby followed Gabe out into the sunlight, grateful to be out of the metaphysical stench of the Mystic Spirit.

"It looks like we've got a lead to track down," Ruby said as she slipped into the backseat of the waiting deputy's vehicle.

CHAPTER TEN

The man placed his eye to the telescope again and watched the couple across the courtyard. The woman was scrubbing a pan, red hot fury in her movements. She was yelling at the man, who stormed red-faced in and out of the room every minute or so. He could not hear what they were saying, but it didn't matter. He enjoyed the silent theater of their mundane lives.

The couple fought a lot. She was always cooking, cleaning, and moving about like it'd kill her to sit still. He was only home in the evening, always coming in late for dinner. It was amusing to watch them wallow in unhappiness, rats on a wheel they could jump off any time but just continued running instead.

He moved the telescope to the apartment to the left where a man in his early twenties was doing burpees. He'd been doing high intensity interval workouts over the last few days, which was new. Normally, the man lifted weights or jumped rope. He had the build of an athlete or perhaps someone who was currently or had been in the military. He was new to the complex, and so far, he wasn't very interesting.

Finally, the man repositioned the spyglass on the apartment to the right of the couple. A woman in her late thirties or early forties was asleep on a plush, emerald-green couch. Her long, blonde hair was piled into a messy bun on top of her head as she held a book to her chest. She must've fallen asleep reading again. He could watch her sleep for hours, and sometimes he did. She was the most interesting show of the three.

The man checked the laptop next to him. The data was still loading. He went back to watching the sleeping woman. He could tell she was lonely. Her roommate or partner had moved out a week ago, and the place seemed to just swallow her whole now that she was alone. He liked having her all to himself. It better prepared him for when they would meet in real life. He memorized her expressions, her movements, everything about her.

She was a Botticelli painting in casual ware, someone others overlooked in the fray. But he saw her. He saw the way her head tossed back when she laughed and her whole body shook with joy. She embodied warmth and light, things he wanted so much to have himself. Instead, he would just take them from her.

The laptop pinged, grabbing the man's attention away from his muse. With a few keystrokes, an automated British male voice began to read off information.

"Forty-one. Five-foot-seven. 194 pounds. Hair: blonde. Eyes: green. Single. No siblings. Parents deceased. Closest living relative is a maternal aunt in Colorado."

He listened to the steady hum of the robotic tone, soaking up every bit of information it said. It wasn't her turn, yet, but he knew she would be his favorite. He continued listening to the information on his next target, soaking in everything about her that he could.

Only a few more days left. He couldn't wait.

CHAPTER ELEVEN

Back at the local police station, Ruby and Gabe had set up a temporary office so they could try to scavenge information about their two new suspects. The local PD wasn't thrilled by their presence, but they needed someplace nearby to convene. One of the office personnel brought them a list of all the people in Daisy's building so they could find this mysterious "Neighbor." Ruby took the first page, and Gabe took the second.

It seemed like hours before either of them came up for air.

"Any luck?"

Ruby shook her head. "So far, just old ladies with tiny dogs and families with small children. I don't think this guy's profile fits either demographic."

Gabe raised his eyebrows in surprise.

"What?"

"Ruby Hunter's got jokes? Who knew?"

"Obviously not you."

They both chuckled. Ruby was too tired to worry if she was letting her guard down too much. She'd drunk so much rotgut coffee that she wasn't sure if she was still awake because the caffeine was so strong or because of the havoc it was wreaking on her system.

"We should probably get something to eat."

Ruby wondered if she'd said something out loud about food and didn't realize it or if Gabe was just hungry too. "Yeah, we're gonna be here a while."

Gabe got up and left the room to find some delivery menus while Ruby continued sifting through the names and information of Daisy's neighbors. Cross-checking every name manually was tedious and frustrating. Just when Ruby thought they had gotten ahead with the two leads, the lack of technology in this small town seemed to thrust them back into the 1980s.

"You want pizza or Chinese?" Gabe asked from the doorway.

"Chinese. Dumplings, fried rice, and chicken wings if they have them."

Gabe smiled at how decisive Ruby was about food. It was one of the only areas of her life where she was confident about what she wanted. Everything else was a guessing game.

When Gabe returned, he had the food with him. Ruby looked up at the clock, wondering how long she'd been going over the list.

"That was fast."

"They didn't have any orders ahead of us."

Gabe divvied up the food and got back to checking his list. Ruby was almost at the end of hers, so she took a break. "So far, my list is a bust."

She decided to eat the fried chicken wings first. They were best when they were hot. Gabe watched as she bit a large chunk of meat out of the first wing.

"What?" she asked, her mouth full of deliciousness.

"Nothing. I am just not used to prim and proper Ruby taking out that chicken wing like a wild cave woman."

Ruby laughed. "I can't help it. I am hungry, and they're my favorite."

"That's fair. Although, poor chicken wing," he smiled.

"And I am not prim and proper all the time, you know."

Ruby wasn't sure why she felt the need to defend herself. He smiled wider, and she smiled back. It was a nice moment, even if Ruby knew it could not last.

No attachments.

Ruby finished off her wings as she watched Gabe absentmindedly load up his chopsticks with Chow Mein. He used the utensils effortlessly, like Asher had. She had never been able to get the hang of them.

"What?" he asked as he caught her staring.

She shook her head, pushing the memory of her and her ex-partner sharing food, in a situation room very like this one. Buckling down to read, she muttered, "Eat your food, Ruiz."

A few minutes later, Ruby noticed something with the last name on her page. She put down her fork and quickly wiped her hands. "I think I've got something. Listen to this. Gregory Harvey moved in across the hall from Daisy six weeks ago. Guess where he moved from?"

Gabe shrugged as he stuck another clump of food in his mouth.

"Prairie, Maryland."

"Wait a minute. Isn't that where the second victim was murdered?"

"Yes, Averie Phelps."

Gabe pushed his food aside. He flipped open his laptop and started typing. "He's got a record."

"What for?"

"Stalking."

Ruby almost dropped her fork. "Let me see."

She read Gregory Harvey's record from top to bottom. He was twenty-nine and had served a two-year sentence for assault and battery. He'd also had four restraining orders against him, all of which were still active.

"What do you think?" Gabe asked her, his voice unsure.

"Well, he's either a patsy, or he's our guy."

"Why do you say that?"

"Naomi Jones, Vallejo's eighth victim, had a stalker in high school. Her record was sealed, and no one but her family knew. Somehow Vallejo knew all the gory details enough to incorporate them into how he killed her."

"Was she the one with the thirteen-threaded rope?"

"No. He kidnapped her and held her in a blackout basement for nineteen days. On the last day, he released thirteen rattlesnakes in the room and left her to die."

"Jesus." Gabe raked his hands down his face. "How do you live with all that garbage in your head?"

"I just do. Someone has to, especially now that he's killing by proxy."

Gabe was quiet for almost a full minute. Ruby wasn't sure if he was trying to decide if he should argue that Vallejo might not be involved or finally accept that she might be right. She didn't know if she should say anything or just let him process everything. She decided to wait and see what he said.

"How the hell does he get his information?"

"Special Agent Carnes thought he might have had connections at a government agency or something, but we never found anything."

"Except it seems like he knows a lot more than anyone could get from somewhere like the Department of Health."

Ruby agreed. She understood how puzzling it all was.

How does Vallejo know what he knows?

"Special Agent Carnes ... Asher told me before he died that Vallejo knew things about him that he'd never told anyone. I never got the chance to find out what he was personally talking about, but Vallejo's also made some comments about things he shouldn't know about me."

"Like what?"

"Just different things, about my past, about my life now. Things he shouldn't know. At first, it was him knowing my parents' names, which is technically public record. Then it was more personal things, like who I was dating for example. I have no idea how he gets his information, or where, but that's how he operates. He finds his way into the deepest, most private crevices of your life and shines a light on all the secrets you thought could never be unearthed."

"Is that why you didn't want me to go with you to see him?"

"His focus is on me, and that's where I need it to stay."

Ruby didn't mean to sound as harsh as she did, but it wasn't a topic she was willing to discuss. Yes, she was protecting Gabe, but that was only because she knew all too well how badly things could go if she didn't.

Gabe sighed as he looked at his watch. Ruby met his eyes and knew instantly he was thinking the same thing. It wasn't too late to talk to a potential suspect.

They both stood up, grabbed their things, and headed to find the nearest deputy to take them to Gregory Harvey's apartment.

CHAPTER TWELVE

Gregory Harvey's apartment building was only eight minutes from the police station. It was a brick building with four floors. Ruby wasn't sure about the town's history, but the building looked like it'd been around since at least the mid-1900s. All she knew was that she hoped there was an elevator. She was dead on her feet from the hike earlier.

The doors to the lobby opened without a code, key card, or key fob. Ruby was surprised at the lack of security, but then again, she lived in a much larger city. The lobby had brass mailboxes on each side, a closed door marked "Office," a stairwell, another closed door marked "Exit," and an elevator. Ruby sighed with relief. Little victories.

Ruby hit the "4" button and watched the doors close. The elevator was rickety and loud, like it might not make it to the second floor, much less the fourth. Ruby immediately checked the date on the certificate of operation.

Three months ago. It should be fine, right?

"I hate elevators," Gabe mumbled.

"Same."

The hallway out of the elevator was lit by ornate wall lanterns, the kind Ruby had seen in hotels that cost a minimum of four hundred dollars per night. Plus tax.

The lighting didn't fit in with the industrial carpet, which looked like it belonged more in a movie theater than an apartment building with its loud colors and repeating patterns.

Ruby took note of the scuff marks on the beige walls. She wondered if they were caused by moving mishaps or something more. Like many of the towns Vallejo had terrorized, Parkville didn't have much of a crime rate. Petty theft, bar fights, typical stuff. Ruby was overly suspicious of anyone and everything. Thanks to Vallejo, she saw malice everywhere.

"This is it. Apartment M."

"Of course it is," Ruby rolled her eyes.

"What do you mean?"

"The letter 'm' is the thirteenth letter in the alphabet."

Gabe raised his eyebrows but didn't say anything. Then, he briskly knocked on the door while Ruby stood back, ready to pull her weapon if necessary. No answer. Gabe knocked again, only harder. It was too early for Gregory Harvey to have gone to bed already.

Ruby caught a flicker of movement from under the door as if someone was standing in front of it and had moved away. She nudged Gabe and tilted her head down to direct him toward the shadows under the door. Someone was definitely inside Gregory Harvey's apartment.

"This is the FBI. We need to speak with Gregory Harvey. Open this door right now."

Ruby made sure her tone was firm, and her voice was loud as she issued the warning to whomever was behind that door to open up or else. They waited thirty seconds, but nothing happened. Ruby nodded at Gabe, giving the go ahead to do what he loved best. She saw a faint smile spread across his lips as he stood back, braced himself, and launched his foot into the door.

Ruby and Gabe piled in through the doorway, weapons drawn. A tall, thin man looked back over his shoulder as he typed something on his laptop.

"FBI! Freeze!" Gabe shouted at the perp. The man didn't stop whatever he was doing. Instead, he worked faster. Ruby realized he was deleting files and quickly charged the man. She hit him hard enough with her shoulder to knock him away from the computer, but not much else. Ruby immediately pointed her gun at him to keep him from trying to get back to the laptop.

The man scoffed at her, like this was all some kind of joke, and put his hands up. He'd clearly been through this before.

CHAPTER THIRTEEN

Sitting across from Gregory Harvey didn't feel the same as the other interrogations. He was relaxed, and his body language was open and inviting. His voice was even and calm as he answered Ruiz's questions. Ruby knew Gregory Harvey had been down this road a few times, but everything about him was far too casual, like he didn't have a care in the world.

"We know you were watching her."

"I have no idea what or who you mean, sir."

Gregory Harvey wasn't being flippant by formerly addressing Special Agent Ruiz. He was being genuinely polite and respectful. Ruby scrutinized every movement and any change to his demeanor, but this perp was as cool as a cucumber in a subzero refrigerator.

"Mr. Harvey, why were you deleting files off of your laptop instead of opening the door?"

"Honestly, ma'am, I was concerned my pornographic browser history could be offensive, especially when I heard your voice on the other side of the door."

"Offensive how?" Gabe took over. Ruby didn't mind. She didn't know if it was because she was exhausted or they were finally getting into a rhythm, but she was completely fine with his tag-team approach.

"In general. I haven't met too many ladies in my life who appreciate pornography the way I do."

Something was off. His supposed efforts to shield Ruby from being offended were derailing their questions.

"Let's start over, Mr. Harvey. Do you know this woman?" Ruby asked as she held up Daisy Hauser's DMV photo.

"Oh yes. That poor girl. She was one of my neighbors. She lived across the hall."

"Did you ever interact with her?"

"Only to say hello in passing or help her with her groceries from time to time. She was very sweet, always smiling. May I?"

Ruby handed him the photo. Gregory Harvey's movements were gentle and easy as he eyed the photo. His eyes lingered a little too long in Ruby's opinion. She put her hand out for him to return the picture.

He narrowed his eyes at her for just a moment before giving it back. It was like she was interrupting something, *intruding*. She found his expression more curious than anything else.

A light knock drummed against the interrogation room door. Gabe got up and checked what it was about. Ruby decided to continue questioning Gregory Harvey.

"Do you know anyone who would have wanted to harm Miss Hauser, Gregory?"

"No, not that I can think of. I believe she was in school or something because she seemed to get home around the same time during the weekdays. And I saw her go out at night a couple times. Maybe she had a boyfriend or something."

Ruby noted the man's change of tone on the word *boyfriend.*

"You seem to know a lot about Daisy for someone who just moved in, who only saw her in passing."

"Just neighborly observations, ma'am. Nothing more."

Gabe returned to his chair with a manila file. He opened the file and spread out several photos. They were video stills of several women in different stages of undress. At first, Ruby thought the women might've been posing for him. Then she realized the women in the photos had no idea anyone was watching, much less recoding them. Including Daisy Hauser.

"Is this your definition of 'neighborly observations,' Mr. Harvey?"

Gregory Harvey started to say something, but then clamped his mouth shut. Ruby looked at each photo. The women were all in apartments similar to Daisy Hauser's.

"Did these women know you were recording them?"

Ruby already knew the answer to Gabe's question. She didn't need to hear it from Gregory Harvey. Every single woman was oblivious to the camera in the room.

"It says here you temporarily worked in maintenance for the building. Is that how you got the cameras in their homes?"

"I am handy, and I needed the work. They needed help and were willing to give me a discount on my rent. Last I checked that wasn't illegal, *sir*."

Ruby looked up from the photos. The man's brow furrowed with irritation, a slight sheen developing across it. Ruby watched him fold his arms tightly around him, a wayward attempt to protect himself. She looked at Gabe, who had stilled next to her. She could tell he was getting angry. They were going in circles.

"Recording individuals in the privacy of their homes without their consent *is illegal*, Mr. Harvey. Given your previous run-ins with the law and your probation status, I am fairly confident you're aware of that distinction. Am I right?"

Ruby watched Gregory Harvey crumble as she spoke. She had to give it to him, he'd lasted longer than she expected.

"I didn't do anything to that girl. I just like ... to watch. That's all. The last time I saw her, she was alive and talking on her cell phone in the hallway. She'd had a bunch of grocery totes in her hands and was trying to get her door open. I came out and offered to help, but she turned me down. She finally got the door open and shut it in my face. That's it. That's all I know, I swear."

The words came out of his mouth like hot lava. Desperation to be believed oozed out with every syllable.

"Did you hear who she was talking to on the phone?" Gabe asked, hoping he could point them in the right direction.

"Probably the guy she was dating. Harold. Harris. I don't know."

"Is there anything else you want to add?"

"I didn't hurt Daisy. Yes, I liked watching her, liked seeing who she was. But I never touched her. All I do is watch. And I can prove it. I am stuck in my apartment all day working remotely for an IT company, which heavily monitors its employees by keystrokes and mouse movement. Every minute I am working, every second I am logged in, is accounted for by some backend program. Not even a person. This ... *this* is the closest I get to actual human interaction."

Gregory Harvey tapped the photos emphatically, as if spying on women was totally normal for a guy in his situation.

"Thank you for your assistance, Mr. Harvey. We'll let the local sheriff take things over from here."

Ruby stood up and walked out of the interrogation room. Gregory Harvey wasn't their guy. Like others before him, he was just another diversion. The only question Ruby had was, did the killer plan this distraction, or was it just pure coincidence?

CHAPTER FOURTEEN

The last thing Ruby wanted to do was spend another minute in Parkville. Unfortunately, that's exactly what they were going to do.

There was still hope that Harrison Cole, Daisy's boyfriend, might wake up. But no promises.

It reminded her how little they had to go on with this case, even though they already had three dead women.

The deputy dropped Ruby and Gabe off at the local Holiday Inn and said he'd be back to get them in the morning. They thanked him for his help. He just nodded as if it was just another day in Parkville. Within fifteen minutes, they were checked in.

Ruby's room was across the hall from Gabe's. It had two queen sized beds, an armchair, a mini fridge, a microwave, a drip coffee maker, a large flatscreen TV, a desk with a chair pushed in, and a full bath. It was one of the nicer places she'd stayed in when working on a case. She figured it was also likely the best accommodations in town.

Ruby started to get undressed when she heard a light rapping at her door. She rebuttoned her blouse and checked the peep hole. It was Gabe.

"What's up?" she asked as she opened the door.

"I just wanted to coordinate with you for tomorrow."

"Oh, um, okay. Come in."

Gabe passed Ruby as she closed the door behind him. He pulled out the desk chair and sat down.

"What time did you want to get started?"

"I don't know. Seven? Eight?"

"Do you want to grab breakfast first? It's included with the rooms."

Ruby grinned. It seemed like Gabe Ruiz was always thinking about food.

"What?" Gabe asked, leaning back in the chair.

"I feel like you plan your life around food."

"The last time I checked food is a requirement for living."

"Yeah, I suppose it is. Let's meet downstairs at seven-thirty and call the deputy at eight. Does that work for you?"

Gabe nodded as he stood up. "See you in the morning, Hunter."

Ruby followed Gabe to the door. He turned to say something to her as he passed the threshold, but instead he just tipped his head at her. She watched him enter his room, then shut her door. Ruby turned the dead bolt and slid the chain across for the added security.

Within a few minutes, Ruby had passed out, fully clothed, on the queen bed farthest from the door.

*

Ruby awoke to the repeated vibration of her phone underneath her. For a second, she had no idea where she was or what time it was. She pulled the phone out from under her and blinked her eyes a few times until the name on the caller ID was clear.

Cursing under her breath, Ruby answered the phone.

"Hunter," her voice croaked with sleep.

"I have been trying to get in touch with you, Agent Hunter. I want a status report right *now*."

Murphy. She sat up, instantly awake.

"Sorry sir, we don't have the best reception up here. We're still tracking a few things down, but ..."

"Do you have any leads, or are you just wasting the Bureau's time and money?"

"We have one lead to follow-up on today and then ..."

"And then you'll be on a plane back to Quantico. Correct?"

"Yes sir."

"I don't know what you and Bellisario have cooked up, but I have got my eye on you, Hunter. You're the exact reason the Bureau needs oversight. You don't *listen* to your superiors, and if you don't watch it, you won't have to because you won't work here anymore. Understand?"

"Yes sir."

Ruby felt her face flush with anger as Executive Assistant Director Barrett Murphy continued to berate her. She wanted to scream and shout back at him, tell him how useless he was, how he'd never solved a worthwhile case in his life, and didn't know what it took to do what she did. Barrett Murphy was nothing more than a spoiled DC politician masquerading as a man of the law, and they both knew it.

But Ruby stayed quiet as he yelled at her. His voice was almost screechy he was so angry. Ruby imagined the reddish-purple color blooming across his face as he continued reprimanding her like a child.

Maybe a blood vessel would burst, and he'd stroke out before he could say another word. Ruby scolded herself for the antagonistic thought. Barrett Murphy didn't deserve to die for being a jerk, much like he didn't deserve to be Executive Assistant Director just because he had connections.

Did he ever yell at men the way he was hollering at her? She doubted it. She knew by the way he treated her that he thought she was the weakest link. And yet, she had been the one who single-handedly brought Vallejo down. Yes, she knew Vallejo *let* her, but Barrett Murphy didn't know that. Ruby wasn't sure why Murphy hated her so much, but she also wasn't sure she cared.

"Don't you *ever* disobey a direct order from your superior again, Special Agent Hunter. You don't have the clearance to understand the problems you've caused with your little visits. Stay away from Vincent Vallejo. Am I clear?"

"Yes sir."

The Executive Assistant Director disconnected the call without another word. Ruby checked the time on her phone. It wasn't even six a.m. She rolled over onto her back and took a deep breath. She wanted to scream until her voice gave out, but she knew that'd probably alarm the guests in the neighboring rooms if there were any.

Ruby covered her face with a pillow and let out a frustrated growl like she was in a 90s death metal band. She was so sick of Murphy and his oversight. She was the one who'd busted Vallejo, so she should be able to talk to him any time she wanted. After all, interviewing serial killers was one of the BAU's main priorities, and who better to interview than the Lucky 13 Killer?

Ruby dragged herself out of bed and into the bathroom. She looked like death warmed over. Maybe a hot shower would help.

As she washed off the sweat and muck of the day before, she could not help but wonder what Barrett Murphy was talking about. What problems could she have caused talking to Vallejo? Technically, he'd helped them catch two different serial killers. She understood that wasn't something he'd want the public to know, but why was he so riled up about it? And why would she need special clearance to know whatever he knew?

Ruby decided Murphy was full of it. He liked to throw around his position in an effort to compensate for how worthless he was. No one knew more about Vincent Vallejo than she did, especially not some self-entitled, overpaid bureaucrat who'd spent all of two months in the field.

Ruby knew what she was doing. That's what frustrated her the most. She kept letting Vallejo derail her investigation, and it had to stop. She needed to make her experience with Vallejo work *for* her, not against her.

With that thought, she had an idea. Ruby finished up her shower and got dressed. She still had over an hour before she was scheduled to meet Gabe for breakfast. She might as well make use of the downtime.

Ruby pulled out her laptop and started looking through Vallejo's old case files. The killer's MO was an obvious reference to Vallejo's 7th victim, but he also seemed to be familiar with other Vallejo victims. Ruby didn't believe it was a coincidence that their first suspect had a history of stalking.

Vallejo was an expert at misdirection. Ruby felt confident that if he'd somehow managed to share the details of his kills with his followers, he must have also shared his strategy and tactics with them. Jared Reuben and Aaron Rodney had actively steered the investigations awry. It was like they had taken the time to pick out red herrings almost as painstakingly as they had their victims.

Ruby knew Vallejo's communications in or out of Boone Correctional Facility had been shut down. The warden had personally guaranteed her that he would make sure the restrictions were heavily enforced. But what if Vallejo had already made contact with his followers? Maybe *that* was what they were missing. Ruby decided it was time to give the warden a call.

Ruby dialed the number to the correctional facility and asked to speak to the warden. Less than ten seconds later, she was connected to Percy Woodward.

"Hello, Agent Hunter. What can I help you with today?" His voice was pleasant and singsong, relaxed as if he didn't have a care in the world. It was strange to think this was the same man who was in charge of a maximum-security prison, housing the worst kinds of criminals.

"Hello, Warden Woodward. Thank you for taking my call. I know you've gone to great lengths to see Vallejo doesn't have any contact with the outside world."

"Yes, per your request, all communications for Vincent Vallejo have been stopped. Nothing comes in, nothing goes out."

"Would you mind please checking to see if there were any communications *prior* to the ban he might've sent or received? We suspect he was in contact with someone before we shut the comms down."

"He's gotten a lot of mail over the last few years. We go through every piece, but it'd be helpful if you could give me something more to go on. Any ideas where the mail could have come from?"

Ruby looked up the locations for the three victims. "I have got three possible locations, so I am thinking anyone within fifty miles of each town."

"Okay, I'll take the location information whenever you're ready."

"Parish, Virginia. Prairie, Maryland. And the last one is Parkville, Ohio."

"All Ps?" the warden asked just as Ruby had the same realization.

"Yes."

"Let me look into it. I'll get back to you as soon as I have something."

Ruby thanked the warden, and they said their goodbyes. How did she and Gabe miss that all the towns started with the letter "P"? And what was the connection to Lucky 13?

What else could they have missed?

CHAPTER FIFTEEN

Gabe was already sitting at a table with a heap of food in front of him when Ruby arrived. She checked her phone, worried she was late. She wasn't. Gabe was just early.

She set things down and headed over to the breakfast bar. Ruby wasn't super hungry, but she knew she needed fuel and lots of caffeine. It was going to be another long day. She plopped some scrambled eggs on her plate, picked up three pieces of bacon, added two sausage links, and rounded out her breakfast with two pieces of toast.

Ruby sat down across from Gabe who smiled as he took a large bite out of a cream cheese loaded bagel. She wondered how many trips he'd already made to the buffet. She unrolled her silverware and placed the cloth napkin in her lap as she looked around. One other couple sat a few tables other, thankfully too far away to eavesdrop. Ruby hated discussing work in public, but some things could not wait.

"I've got some news ..."

"Me too," Gabe interrupted. Given his excited state, it must be good news.

"Okay. What's up?"

"Harrison Cole, the boyfriend, is awake from his coma, and he's talking. Apparently, he arrived just as the killer was finishing off the victim and tried to stop him. The suspect beat him to a pulp before dragging him back to the parking lot. The kid was left unconscious on a bench outside of the emergency room four hours before hikers found Daisy's body."

"Can we go talk to him?"

Ruby hadn't expected this development. What if Harrison could identify the killer? They might *finally* be ahead for once, especially if the killer thought Harrison was dead.

"We can head over there after breakfast. What about you?"

"Oh, a couple things actually. Did you notice all the towns start with the letter 'P'?"

"How did we miss that?"

"Beats me. Too busy focusing on other things?"

"Yeah, there's no shortage of evidence to comb through with three victims, is there?"

Ruby nodded and took a bite of her food. She made a mental note to check the three case files again.

"The other thing is I called the warden at Boone Correctional Facility. I know they stopped all comms in and out, which got me thinking. What if he was talking to someone *before* we shut all that down?"

"Ruby …"

"Just listen, okay?"

Gabe nodded and ate some more of his bagel. Ruby took a sip of coffee and leaned in.

"They found someone. A woman named Fernanda Torres has had an ongoing correspondence with Vallejo for over two years. Obviously not anymore, but still ..."

"Seriously? Where do these people come from?"

Ruby shrugged and drank some more coffee. She wasn't hungry, but she knew they were going to be too busy to stop for food later. She added a couple of pieces of bacon to her toast and scraped some scrambled eggs on top. She smushed the sides together to make a pseudo breakfast sandwich.

"Where is this Fernanda Torres located?"

Ruby covered her mouth as she chewed so she could answer Gabe. "Greenacres, Virginia. About fifty miles from the first victim."

*

Gabe called the deputy to pick them up while Ruby checked out. A few minutes later, they were on their way to see Harrison Cole.

Parkville Medical Center was a sprawling three-story, concrete building with a main entrance lined with trees and an emergency room entrance directly off the street. It looked much newer than Daisy Hauser's apartment building, but not so recent it stuck out against the surrounding architecture.

The deputy accompanied them inside, flashing his badge as needed. Ruby appreciated the escort. It made it a lot easier for them to do their jobs and avoid some of the red tape.

They walked straight to the elevators. The deputy punched the button for the third floor and then tapped the "close door" button repeatedly. Gabe looked at Ruby like he was about to punch the deputy in the back of the head. Ruby smirked but resisted the urge to laugh.

The deputy introduced them to the head nurse. Ruby and Gabe identified themselves and asked if they could speak with Harrison Cole.

"Of course. His family is here with him. He's doing much better. Follow me."

Ruby and Gabe followed the nurse down the hall to where two armed policemen stood, one on each side of a closed door. The nurse pushed the door open and held it for them to enter. Ruby noticed the deputy hadn't come with them. She looked back at the nurse's station and saw he was talking to a pretty woman behind the desk. It was probably for the best. They didn't need him interfering with their investigation.

"Mr. and Mrs. Cole, this is Special Agent Hunter and Special Agent Ruiz with the FBI. They're here to speak with Harrison."

The nurse gestured Gabe and Ruby forward before she turned and left the room.

Mr. Cole sat on the left side of Harrison's bed while Mrs. Cole sat on the right. Both looked exhausted and haggard, just as Ruby would. Harrison's face was still swollen and bruised. Even through the bandages, his nose looked like it had been pulverized, and his neck was in a brace. The young man looked like he'd been in a horrible car accident, like a machine had done this to him. Not another human.

How could one person do so much damage?

"We apologize for interrupting, but we're investigating what happened to Daisy Hauser. We wanted to speak with you if you're up to it. Anything you remember could be a big help."

"He already spoke to the police. Can't you just leave him be?" Mrs. Cole pleaded. Harrison groaned as he moved his hand to his mother's arm.

"I don't ... remember ... much. But I'll tell you what I can." Harrison's voice was hoarse and filled with pain. Ruby could tell by the short breaths he was taking that he must've had a few broken ribs or something. It was hard for him to say more than a few words at a time.

"Would it be okay if we spoke with Harrison alone?" Gabe asked. Mr. Cole nodded and beckoned his wife to join him in the cafeteria. She hesitated, terrified to leave her son alone.

"It's ... fine, Mom."

Mr. Cole guided Mrs. Cole out of the room, a sob echoing in the hallway she'd no doubt been holding in for far too long. Ruby could not imagine how horrible it'd been for them to sit by his bed, waiting for him to wake up and knowing there wasn't anything they could do. She felt like that was the only reason the killer had left Harrison alive. Tormenting Harrison's family was probably almost as satisfying as killing Daisy. One lasted a hell of a lot longer, that's for sure.

"Harrison, can you share with us anything you remember?"

Ruby and Gabe sat down where Mr. and Mrs. Cole had been seated only moments earlier. Gabe pulled out a notepad and took notes while Ruby asked some questions.

Harrison struggled through labored breathing. "A lot of it's fuzzy. I was supposed to meet Daisy at Orion's Lookout at 11 p.m., that way we could see the constellations clearly. But I'd gotten held up at work. I thought I'd be just a few minutes late, but then I hit every red light on the way there.

"As I got out of my car, I heard a scream coming from the top of the trailhead. At the time, I thought Daisy might've gotten freaked out by a snake or something. I ran up the trail to make sure she was okay. When I got to the opening, I saw a large shape—I think it was a man—standing over something on the ground." He swallowed. "As I got closer, I realized that thing on the ground was Daisy."

His face fell, and he sniffed.

"What happened then?"

"I thought she'd had an asthma attack or something and the man was trying to help her. She got those from time to time and didn't always have her inhaler. When I was just a few feet away, I saw the rope, and it all came into focus. The man hadn't been trying to help Daisy; he was strangling her. I shouted for the man to get away from her, but he didn't budge. I thought I'd call the police, but I didn't have my cell—it had either fallen out in the car or on the trail. So, I did the only thing I could and started running back to my car, screaming every step of the way. I—"

"You didn't try to stop him?" Ruby asked.

He gave her a wounded look. "I know I should've. I panicked. He looked really big. There are usually rangers and local police, so I thought maybe I could get *somebody's* attention.

"But just as I reached his car, someone grabbed me by the shoulders and threw me to the ground. I must have hit my head, but that's the last thing I remember before waking up here," he said. "I am not sure why he didn't kill me too. He almost did. They had to keep me in a medically induced coma for twenty-two days to give my body time to heal."

Ruby asked, "Is there anything about the man that was familiar?"

"No, nothing. He was a complete stranger."

"Do you remember anything else physical about him?"

"He was just very large ... and really strong. I am six-one, but this guy just seemed like an ogre, he was so big. I knew there was no way I could fight him."

"Did he say anything while all this was happening?"

"Not that I recall ... wait, yes. He did. He said something ... about the stars and the moon. It didn't make any sense, but he said it over and over again. Like a mantra or something."

"Was it familiar to you?"

"No, I'd never heard it before. It sounded like something you'd find ... in a fortune cookie. The stars still shine with the moon ... or I don't know. I honestly can't remember. I'm sorry." He held his head. "I'm not so good anymore. In the head."

"Harrison, you have nothing to apologize for. You've already given us so much, and it was really brave of you to try and help Daisy."

As Ruby stood up, she saw a tear roll down his cheek. He didn't move to wipe it away or hide it. He just let it go. Ruby gently squeezed Harrison's hand, careful not to hurt him, hoping to comfort him in some small way.

"Thank you for talking with us, Harrison," Gabe said warmly. The two men made eye contact for a moment, but what passed between them seemed like something more. What, Ruby had no idea, but she imagined it was some sort of moment of respect. She could tell Gabe understood Harrison did a lot more in his situation than most would. It was surprising the killer left him alive.

Gabe wished Harrison well and left the room. He was never all that comfortable with interviewing victims. Unfortunately, if he was going to stay in this business long, he needed a stronger stomach for these kinds of things.

"Ma'am?"

Ruby turned as Harrison called out to her.

"Wait. I guess I didn't pass out right away. I remember ... he also said something after he dumped me ... outside."

"Oh yeah?"

"He leaned down and whispered that it just wasn't my time yet. That the stars weren't aligned. I couldn't see anything but when he drove away, I heard him honk the car horn several times. It was like he wanted to make sure someone found me."

"Maybe he did. The thing about people like this guy is that they're never all bad."

"I wish ... he would've just let me die."

Harrison's face crumpled with pain and grief. She wondered if this was the first time that he'd had a chance to break down and let go. He'd been through so much, but maybe he hadn't really talked about it until now.

Ruby walked over to where Gabe had been sitting and swiped a couple of tissues from a tissue box on a nearby table. She dabbed it gently next to each of his eyes, careful to avoid any of the bruised areas.

"It's okay you feel that way, Harrison. It's okay that you're angry and sad and confused. This person took things from you that you'll never get back, but you'll get through this. I am speaking from personal experience, so please hear me when I say to you that you will be okay. Maybe not today or tomorrow, but it will happen. All right?"

Harrison gave the slightest nod as more tears slid down the sides of his face. Ruby squeezed his hand once more. "Thank you, Harrison."

Then she looked at Gabe, not articulating what she was thinking. But he frowned and nodded at her as if he understood completely.

This is one of them. One of Vallejo's minions.

CHAPTER SIXTEEN

It took the rest of the day for Ruby and Gabe to wrap up their investigation with the local police. They were far from solving the case, but it was their responsibility to share the information they had and what they had been able to put together so far for the killer's profile.

They were confident he was a white male in his late twenties or early thirties. He was at least six-foot-three and over 200 pounds. He worked with his hands and was most likely a trade worker who could pick up and move whenever he needed.

Ruby left out the part that he was also likely an avid Vallejo follower. She hadn't found concrete proof linking the two, but she was hoping Fernanda Torres would be able to fill in some of those blanks.

Their flight to Virginia was delayed due to some nasty weather sweeping across the Ohio River Valley toward Pittsburgh. Ruby was ready to get out of Parkville. She'd hoped she would be able to sleep in her own bed, but it didn't look like that was going to happen.

Gabe and Ruby sat in the lounge of the private airport waiting for the weather to clear so they could leave. Gabe was looking at something on his laptop while Ruby reviewed her notes from the trip. She had a mild headache and didn't want to make it worse by staring at a computer screen.

"I have looked through every famous quote website I could find, and so far, I have only come across three that mention both the moon and the stars. And none of them sound like a mantra this guy would be repeating as he's beating the snot out of someone."

"Okay. What are they?"

"The first one is 'Shoot for the moon because even if you miss, you'll land among the stars.' There are multiple variations, but that's the gist."

"Yeah, that seems kind of long and fairly common. I feel like Harrison could have recognized that one if it was the right one."

"Possibly. I am not a big quote person, but I have heard that one a few times in my life. The second one is 'You can be the moon and still be jealous of the stars.'"

"The jealousy angle seems off. I guess it could work if it was the unsub's own version of it. And the last one?"

"Unless he's jealous of Vallejo?"

Ruby was stupefied. Had Gabe Ruiz really just suggested a Vallejo angle?

"I'm sorry, what did you say?"

"You heard me."

"Okay, tell me the last one please."

"'Moonlight drowns out all but the brightest stars.'"

"Hmm. Who was that one by?"

"J.R.R. Tolkien."

Ruby's breath hitched in her throat.

"What?"

"Vallejo was teaching a special topics course called *The Psychology of Christianity in Middle Earth* when we arrested him."

Ruby remembered how proud Vallejo was that he'd gotten the Dean to approve the course, given Tolkien's ties to Fantasy. She imagined he'd thought of himself as a sort of Tolkien figure, creator of worlds and complicated mythology. To Ruby, he was more of one of Tolkien's monstrous characters than Tolkien himself.

"Look, Hunter, I get that I could not possibly understand your experiences with Vincent Vallejo and how they've shaped your life over the last three plus years. But I'm concerned that you keep finding connections to him with every case. I'm not saying you're wrong or anything. It's just not every murderer is a Vallejo follower."

Ruby wasn't sure how to respond. She didn't *want* every case to be connected to Vallejo. So far, though, they had been.

"I don't think every murderer is one of his followers, Ruiz. But the last two have had a connection to the Lucky 13 Killer, and it's quite possible this one does too. I'm not trying to tie them to Vallejo, but I'm also not going to ignore obvious connections."

"I just don't want us to get so wrapped up in the Vallejo angle that we miss the forest for the trees. If you know what I mean."

Ruby nodded in agreement. She knew exactly what he meant, and she didn't blame him for not wanting to be dragged into a Vallejo spiral if it wasn't absolutely necessary. Ruby refocused her attention on her notes while Gabe went back to trying to find more quotes about the moon and stars.

After what seemed like just a few minutes, an airline attendant approached them.

"Special Agent Hunter? Special Agent Ruiz? We'll be ready for takeoff in fifteen."

"Okay, thank you," Gabe said as he stretched.

"What time is it?" Ruby asked, taking a moment to stretch herself.

"A little after four a.m."

"Oh wow. I had no idea. Did you find anything else?"

"Not really, but I do think you were onto something with the Tolkien reference."

Ruby raised her eyebrows; not sure she'd heard Gabe correctly.

"Tell me more, please."

"I thought you'd like that," he teased. "So, I cross-referenced a few things. It turns out there are a lot of message boards devoted to Vallejo, not that that's surprising at all."

"People are gross."

"You're not wrong. Anyway, the internet is a rabbit hole of information, conspiracy theories, and madman ramblings."

"I know what the internet is, Gabe."

"Right, sorry. The thing is that I found something. Apparently, Vallejo wrote a paper when he first started teaching specifically on the celestial imagery in Tolkien's work. It was a little highbrow and convoluted, but he spent a lot of time analyzing that quote. Then, he talked about how we know, based on modern astronomy, that the moon gets its light from the sun and the sun is a star, so stars are the brightest light in the universe."

"So, in other words, the moon can't outshine the stars?"

"Exactly."

"Okay, but how does that relate to this case?"

"I am still working on that part."

"I think we both need some sleep."

Ruby and Gabe boarded their flight a few minutes later. The flight attendant went through his safety spiel and let them know it'd be a three-hour flight. He also advised they could dim the lights and provide both snacks and blankets. Ruby opted for both.

Ruby shifted in her seat until she found a comfortable position. Once she did, she looked over at Gabe, and he was already asleep.

Too easily. She didn't know how he could do that. All she could think about was that as they slept, the killer might have been out there, looking to claim his next victim.

CHAPTER SEVENTEEN

Ruby awoke to the flight attendant's voice welcoming them to Charlottesville. She had a horrible crick in her neck from how she slept. Gabe didn't look much better than she felt. Ruby had hoped the three hours would give her a second wind, but instead it just made her more tired.

"I am going to need some coffee as soon as we get to the gate."

"Agreed. I am also going to need some food. Nuts and Belvita breakfast biscuits just don't cut it."

"How are you always hungry?"

"How are you not?"

Ruby sighed and gathered her things. She didn't like to dilly-dally.

Once they deplaned, Ruby detoured to the women's restroom. She needed to change clothes and freshen up before she was stuck in a small space with another human, much less Gabe, all day. Thankfully, she always had an extra change of clothes in her bag along with baby wipes and dry shampoo.

Once a Girl Scout, always a Girl Scout.

Ruby heard the words in her mind as clearly in that moment as she had the day Asher Carnes said them to her. They had been watching Vallejo, hoping to confirm he was the Lucky 13 Killer. He'd matched the profile, but he'd been careful.

Unfortunately, meal breaks weren't factored into surveillance, and Asher was a three-squares-a-day kind of man. When he didn't eat, he got what Ruby liked to call *hangry*.

They were waiting to see if Vallejo left his house on a particular night that they were certain the killer was going to strike based on an anonymous note the killer had sent to the local newspaper. Asher started to get grumpy, so Ruby pulled out a small jar of peanut butter and a pack of saltines from her bag. Then, to his utter delight, she presented him with a three-piece cutlery travel set. That's when he declared, "Once a Girl Scout, always a Girl Scout."

Her memories of Asher were strongest when she was overtired. It was like they were weighted down in her subconscious until she hadn't had enough sleep. Then it was like someone had cut the rope and all the moments they'd shared came rushing back.

Ruby didn't just miss Asher. She missed the life she knew she could have had with him. Everything felt so safe with him, so easy. She never imagined she had lived in a world where he didn't exist and yet here she was.

She always missed Asher the most just after she woke up. For just a moment, she'd forget he was gone. Then she'd open her eyes and find herself alone. Waking up on a plane wasn't any different than waking up in her own bed. She felt his absence everywhere.

Ruby met Gabe at the car rental counter. He handed her a cup of coffee while he finished signing the paperwork for the car. They had decided it was better to have their own vehicle than wait around on local police. Plus, they weren't dealing with a victim. They were dealing with a potential suspect.

Gabe left to go get the car from the lot while Ruby called Bellisario to check-in.

"How's it going?" Bellisario sounded a little worried.

"We found a woman who was corresponding with Vallejo for just over two years before we stopped his comms access. We're hoping she knows something or can at least point us in the right direction."

"Be careful, Hunter. That man seems to inspire the worst in people."

Ruby appreciated Bellisario's concern, but he wasn't telling her anything she didn't already know from firsthand experience. Vallejo's followers were *killing* people, not just acting like he was the second coming of Christ.

"Before you go, I just wanted you to know I spoke with Murphy. He demanded that I not go see Vallejo anymore and said something about me not having clearance to know what my visits to the prison were interfering with."

"You don't report to Murphy, Special Agent Hunter, and I haven't said a word to you about your psychological review of Vincent Vallejo. I do expect you to turn in any notes you might have so we can be sure to share them through official channels as appropriate."

"Yes sir."

On that note, Bellisario wished her good luck and ended the call. Ruby thought it was curious he didn't seem to have a problem with her consulting Vallejo. Maybe he knew it was something she needed to do, especially since his name kept coming up in new cases.

Ruby rubbed the chill from her arms and waited for Gabe. After a few minutes, she pulled her cell phone back out to call him, wondering what was taking him so long. Then he pulled up in a black SUV.

"Kind of obvious, don't you think?" Ruby asked as she got in the passenger side.

"So what. I like the way it drives."

"How far to Greenacres?"

"About forty-five minutes. But before we hop on the interstate, I need sustenance."

"Fine. While you get food, I'll start going through Fran McCormick's file again. It can't be a coincidence his first victim lived so close to Fernanda Torres."

Fifteen minutes later, Gabe pulled onto the highway just as he finished scarfing down the second of two overloaded breakfast sandwiches that he'd gotten from a fast food joint. Ruby ate a couple of plain biscuits. She hadn't had enough sleep for anything heavier.

"I keep going over Fran McCormick's file, but nothing stands out. She also doesn't appear to have had any interest in astrology or astronomy."

"There's something that connects these three women to each other or the killer. There always is. Even with Vallejo. Maybe if he hadn't been so obsessed with the number thirteen, he wouldn't have gotten caught."

"Yeah," Ruby said half-heartedly. She knew the only reason Vallejo got caught was because it was what *he* wanted. Everything had gone according to some grand plan, he even said so when she cornered him. How she wished she could go back in time and put a bullet right between his eyes. Maybe then, the nine women from these three cases would still be alive.

Ruby pushed the "woulda, coulda, shoulda" thoughts from her mind. There was no point in looking back on how things might've been if only she'd done something different. Women were dead, and Ruby hoped, down into the marrow of her bones, that Fernanda Torres would be the lead they needed to finally get ahead. She was so tired of playing catch up with murderers.

Gabe parked on the street in front of 931 Royal Castle Lane, the home of Fernanda Torres. It was a dilapidated, mid-century brick rambler. A run-down, burgundy Oldsmobile sat in front of the garage, and the grass was patchy. In some areas, it was overgrown, and in others, it was burnt to a crisp. Ruby wondered how long Fernanda Torres had lived there.

Ruby rang the doorbell first to see if anyone would answer. When no one did, Gabe knocked loudly. The door nudged open as if the last person who went through it didn't close it all the way.

"Fernanda Torres, this is the FBI. Your name came up in a case we're investigating, and we need to speak with you," Gabe's voice echoed through the house. Ruby wasn't sure anyone was even home.

Gabe drew his weapon and moved into the home. Ruby followed. As he moved off to the right, Ruby stopped in her tracks. There, hanging in the foyer of the home, was a portrait of Vincent Vallejo. It was painted like he was some sort of religious icon and lit from above with a wired portrait lamp.

"Hunter, you've got to see this," Gabe called from the other room. Ruby followed the sound of his voice into what should have been a living room. Instead, the entire room was an elaborate shrine to Vincent Vallejo. Framed photos of all sizes filled with Vallejo's face adorned the mantle above the fireplace. Lit candles filled the space where wood would normally go. Everywhere she looked, there was something referencing Vincent Vallejo. Fernanda Torres's obsession with the man was completely out in the open for everyone to witness. The sight of it all made Ruby want to vomit.

Every inch of wall space was covered in old newspaper articles, crime scene photos, and letters. The newspaper articles featured headlines from Vallejo's twenty-four-month killing spree, many of which Ruby had read herself at the time. They were laminated and taped to the wall as if they were treasured baseball cards.

Ruby knew all sorts of memorabilia was out there for sickos like this, but she hadn't expected to see copies of official crime scene photos. She inspected a couple of letters, but they weren't from Vallejo. They were from other "fans," begging Fernanda to give Vallejo messages like she was some sort of Mary figure in his cult of murderers.

"Hey, come look at this," Ruby called over to Gabe. He was looking at one of the articles about Asher's death. Seeing the headline and Asher's official FBI headshot was like a ten-gauge needle directly to her heart.

"What are those?" he asked as he walked over.

"Letters from fans *to Fernanda* about Vallejo."

"What do you mean 'about Vallejo'?"

"They're pleading with her to give him messages and well wishes. Like she was some sort of go-between or something."

"Maybe she was."

"Let's keep looking. Maybe we'll find something concrete for once."

Gabe nodded and headed toward the kitchen. Everywhere Ruby turned, Vallejo stared back at her. It was beyond unsettling. She drew her weapon and walked slowly down the hall toward the two bedrooms.

Collages of photos adorned the walls of the hallway leading to the back of the home. Ruby glanced at them, thinking they were likely of Fernanda Torres's family. Then she did a double take. Every picture on the wall was a photoshopped image of Vallejo with the same woman, who she assumed must be Fernanda, doing different things. They were at the beach in one, in a snowy cabin in another, fishing on a boat in the last one. It was like nothing she'd ever seen before.

The photos weren't professional or even well done. It was clear they'd been pasted together in a basic program like Paint and then framed. Ruby shuddered at the thought that there were people out there who *fantasized* about living a life with someone like Vincent Vallejo.

The bedrooms weren't any better. One bedroom was full of what looked like case file boxes, all marked with "Vallejo" on them. Ruby made a mental note to have the boxes checked. It concerned her that they looked so official. And if they were, that could mean Fernanda Torres knew someone who had access to records only law enforcement should be able to access.

The second bedroom, or primary bedroom, was also filled with Vallejo's image. To her horror, Ruby noticed a pillow designed to look like a person's head with Vallejo's face handstitched on it. This woman was completely obsessed.

"You find anything back there?" Gabe called out.

"Not anything worthwhile."

Ruby holstered her weapon and headed back toward the front of the home. Just as she did, she heard something shift in the hall closet. Before she could draw her weapon again, the closet door flew open, and a wild-haired woman launched herself at Ruby, screeching like a banshee.

Ruby struggled to keep the woman from clawing and scratching at her. She tried to shout for Gabe's help as she attempted to get away, but the woman's elbow clocked her in the jaw. Hard.

Ruby pushed and shoved, but the woman just kept coming. Ruby tried to call out for Gabe again when suddenly the woman was launched backwards. Gabe pointed his weapon at the woman and told her to stay down.

"You okay?" he asked, glancing over his shoulder at Ruby.

Stroking her jaw, she recentered herself and took a deep, calming breath. "I'll live."

CHAPTER EIGHTEEN

Back at headquarters, Ruby watched Fernanda Torres sit in the interrogation room. Once Gabe had knocked her off of Ruby, she immediately calmed down. She claimed there'd been some break-ins in the area recently, and she thought they were there to rob her.

Now, she was just sitting there. Waiting. Like a perfectly normal person.

"Here. It'll help with the swelling," Gabe said as he handed her an ice pack from the first aid kit.

"Thanks." Ruby gently placed the ice pack on the right side of her face. It throbbed from the blow Fernanda landed in the struggle.

"You ready to go in there?"

"Not really."

"Like you said before, maybe she's the lead we have been looking for."

Ruby sighed and reluctantly followed Gabe into the room. She was so tired of riddles and misdirection. Another woman was going to die in what could be just a matter of days if they didn't figure out a connection or something tangible about the killer that connected him to his victims. At least if they knew how he was selecting his victims, they could possibly find him or the victim in time.

The reality was that Ruby was tired of it all. She knew she needed more sleep, but she never could rest easy when there was an active case. Lately, even that wasn't true thanks to Vallejo. She'd had too many restless nights thinking about how Vincent Vallejo could be the mastermind behind these serial killers, but not much made sense. He was under lock and key, with no communication options available to him with the outside world. She'd found no connection between the killers and Vallejo or the victims and Vallejo except the clues, or whatever they were, that Vallejo had given her along the way.

"Hi Fernanda. Can I get you anything before we get started?"

So far, Gabe was far better at interrogating suspects than he was at talking to victims' families. It made sense in a way. He was trying to trip up the suspects, find the gap in their timelines and stories. With victims' families, all they had after a violent crime was empty spaces where their loved ones should have been. It's never the same, and it's never easy knowing what to say to try and fill those spaces.

"Nothing for me, please," Fernanda smiled. She radiated warmth, which surprised Ruby. It was like a completely different woman was sitting in front of her compared to the ball of rage she had been earlier when she'd attacked Ruby.

"Fernanda, I am Special Agent Ruiz, and this is my partner, Special Agent Hunter."

"It's nice to *officially* meet you both. I am sorry about your jaw, Special Agent Hunter. I hope it doesn't hurt too badly."

Ruby caught something sinister in Fernanda's tone, like she was proud of landing the blow to Ruby's face. Gabe caught it, too, based on the look he gave Ruby. He continued, radiating charm and the "good cop" persona.

"We'd like to know more about you, Fernanda."

"I am an open book, agents."

"How long have you known Vincent Vallejo?"

"Who's that?" She batted her eyes innocently.

Gabe groaned. "The man you have a thousand pictures of in your home."

"That's none of your business."

Ruby exchanged a look with Gabe. "Actually, Fernanda, that's why you're here. We know you were corresponding with him until recently. What did you two write about?"

"It's private."

Ruby noticed how Fernanda blushed each time Gabe asked her a question. She wasn't sure if it's because she was shy, attracted to Gabe, or what. What she was sure of is that they didn't have time to figure out what game she was playing. Ruby got an idea and hoped Gabe would just go with it.

"Special Agent Ruiz, would you mind getting me some water please? I am quite parched after our little … *adventure* earlier."

Gabe nodded and stepped out of the room.

Ruby attempted to smile at Fernanda, but the pulsating ache in her jaw made her flinch. Fernanda caught Ruby's wince, which made her sneer as if she relished Ruby's pain.

"I am not like the others, Special Agent Hunter."

"What do you mean?"

"They blame you. Hate you even. They can't see his genius the way I can."

"Who's 'they'?"

"You don't need me to figure that out," Fernanda smiled again, this time less menacing. "I used to feel the way they did, especially because he talked so much about you. All the time. It was ... difficult in the beginning."

It was clear to Ruby that Fernanda was choosing her words carefully, much like Vallejo would have if he was sitting in front of her.

"I think it would be a challenge for any woman to listen to someone they cared for talk about another woman, regardless of how innocent the relationship might be."

Ruby hated trying to empathize with Fernanda Torres. The truth was that Ruby had zero empathy for her. She was just as sick as the rest of them, worshipping a psychopathic serial killer like Vallejo.

"I wouldn't call the relationship 'innocent,' Special Agent Hunter. He's just as obsessed with you as you are with him."

Ruby felt the heat flush her face before she could stop it. She was *not obsessed* with Vincent Vallejo. She took a slow, quiet, deep breath to calm herself. Otherwise, this interrogation was going off the rails fast.

"I am obsessed with my work, Ms. Torres. Unfortunately, he seems to continue to be relevant to that work even though he's locked away in solitary."

"Don't you understand, Special Agent Hunter? There is no force on earth capable of stopping what he's started. I know it. You know it. We're all just pieces of the puzzle *he* created."

Ruby didn't like how cryptic Fernanda was being. She didn't have the patience for it. She decided to try a different approach.

"How much do you know about his victims?"

"As much as he has allowed. Knowledge is power, after all."

"What did you know about his last victim, Asher Carnes?"

Fernanda shifted slightly in her chair, like she wasn't sure where Ruby was going with her questions. "That he was an FBI agent like you. And your partner. Although, I'd say you've upgraded since then."

Ruby didn't react to Fernanda's comment, which made the woman squirm even more.

"Yes, Special Agent Carnes was my partner. We were also dating. Pretty seriously. Like buy a house together, adopt a dog, and have kids kind of serious. Did Vallejo tell you that?" Ruby asked, already knowing the answer. It was hard for her to admit these things out loud, not just to the deranged woman in front of her, but also to anyone listening on the other side of the glass.

But it worked. Fernanda's discomfort was growing, her calm façade dissolving under the most pedestrian of emotions: jealousy.

"So?"

"So, for his thirteenth and final victim, his pièce de résistance if you will, he killed someone I loved and was planning to spend the rest of my life with. In fact, Special Agent Carnes was with me the night he died, something Vallejo knew. Don't you find it curious he would choose *my* lover as his final victim?"

Fernanda's eyes narrowed as she clenched her jaw. It was like she wanted to argue, to stake her claim for Vallejo, but she could not.

"It's not my place to be curious about Vincent Vallejo's motivations. Everyone has a theory, Special Agent Hunter. But theories aren't facts. However, if I was a betting woman, which I am not, I'd wager your partner's death was more about you than your partner."

"Which only supports my point, Ms. Torres. The way you talk about him, *worship* him, one could easily surmise that you're in love with him. But if he's obsessed with someone else, how could he be in love with you?"

Ruby watched as Fernanda's face filled with an unsettling calmness.

"As some version of the old adage goes, Special Agent Hunter, 'ours is not to reason why, ours is but to do and die.' His full vision has yet to be realized, which I greatly look forward to witnessing. However, you're barking up the wrong tree, as usual."

Ruby counted to ten in her mind, desperate to keep her cool. More riddles. More nonsense. How many more deaths had to happen before the mystery of Vallejo was revealed?

Just as Ruby felt like she could not hold back the raging waters of her anger any longer, Gabe returned with a bottle of water. Their eyes connected, and she knew he understood. He gave her a slight smile and sat down.

"Let's cut to the chase, Fernanda. Three more women are dead and, right now, you're our prime suspect."

She grinned. "Then you aren't doing your jobs very well, are you?"

"We have every reason to believe you're involved with this latest case, especially because of your proximity to one of the victims," Ruby said.

"That may be, but I didn't do it. And you cannot keep me here. I know nothing, and I have an alibi. I was in the Bronx visiting family. Based on the news, none of your victims were in New York. Correct?"

"Convenient," Ruby spit out, her anger simmering too close to the surface.

"I only just got back yesterday. I have been there for the last three months taking care of my four nephews. My brother has cancer, and my sister-in-law needed the help. I am sure you can check traffic cams, CCTV, or whatever, not to mention the wad of receipts in my purse."

Gabe looked at Ruby. Fernanda Torres's interrogation was over.

"Thank you for your time, Ms. Torres," Ruby said in the most professional tone she could muster. Fernanda smiled as Ruby and Gabe stood up to leave.

"I know you want to be the hero and save the next victim, Special Agent Hunter. Vallejo says it's kind of your thing. But you're running out of time. I can't help you because I know nothing. All I know is that this one isn't like the other two. Vallejo made sure of that."

It took Ruby everything she had to walk out of the room without showing the rage she had inside.

CHAPTER NINETEEN

"Please tell me you found something," Ruby asked.

Gabe shook his head.

Ruby pulled a chair up next to him as he scrolled through images on his laptop.

"Tech Ops sent over everything on her phone, and so far, it's just more Vallejo devotion. Her browser history is dedicated to two things: serial killers in general and Vallejo fan pages. Not to state the obvious, but her zealous fidelity to Vincent Vallejo is seriously creepy."

"What about the call and text logs?"

"Let's take a look."

Gabe pulled up the information and they both leaned in to scan the fine print of Fernanda Torres's phone records. Ruby hated looking at information on a laptop. It's not that she hated technology. She understood its usefulness and efficiency better than most. But after she worked with Asher and he insisted on having the paper in his hands, she also understood the limitations of technology.

"Can you print me a copy?"

"Ruby, it's more than a hundred pages."

"Okay. So only print the pages from the dates of the murders. That should waste less trees, right?"

Gabe rolled his eyes.

"How about I grab us some lunch while you do that?" Ruby asked, hoping it would be enough of a "thank you" that she wouldn't have to actually thank him.

"Fine. I want an enchilada-style sweet pork barbacoa burrito with cilantro lime rice, double pintos, and hot roasted red chile sauce from Casa Comida."

"Wow, that's seriously specific. You might want to write that down, Gabe. Otherwise, there's no guarantee that's what you'll get."

"How about I just order it and you pick it up?"

"That's probably a much better plan."

"Do you want anything?"

"Sure, just nothing too spicy."

Ruby decided to walk to Casa Comida. It was only three blocks away, and the sun was out. Asher had always told her to get outside and walk whenever and wherever she could. He'd sworn by it.

It's better for your mind and your body.

Casa Comida had been around for decades. It was one of the best authentic Mexican restaurants in the tri-state area, at least that's what Gabe and a sign in their window said. Ruby wondered if Asher had ever eaten there. All she remembered them eating was takeout. It would have been nice if they could have gone out to dinner, somewhere fancy enough for them both to dress up.

There were so many things she and Asher hadn't gotten to do together, things they'd taken for granted because they'd thought they had more time. They'd talked a lot about what they wanted to do once they caught the Lucky 13 Killer. Take time off, go somewhere tropical, just live their lives as a couple finally. But Vallejo made sure that none of it was ever going to happen.

Ruby pushed opened the door to find a beautiful, modern space with the kitchen area exposed at the back. Butcher block topped tables with seating for two and four people scattered across the room, all with a perfect view to watch the kitchen crew work.

Ruby had always assumed Casa Comida was more of a grab-and-go style restaurant, but that was probably because that's how everyone she knew ate. On the go. It was the one reason she always had a roll of Tums in her purse. She never seemed to have time to fully digest a meal, which was always hard on her body.

"Welcome to Casa Comida. Table for one?" a honey-blonde haired woman with a welcoming smile asked. She didn't even look eighteen.

"Actually, no. I have a pick-up order."

"Perfect. May I have the name please?"

"Gabe Ruiz?"

"Ah, yes. I'll be right back with your food, ma'am."

Ruby thanked the woman, although her first instinct was to correct her for calling her "ma'am." She was still more than a year away from thirty. Hopefully, she didn't look as old as she felt.

"Here you are. May I get you anything else?" the young woman asked politely as she handed over a two-handled paper bag with the restaurant's name across the front. Ruby shook her head and thanked her for her help.

As she walked back to Headquarters, Ruby scolded herself. Based on the hostess's speech patterns, she was just being polite. She had manners, not some sort of nefarious agenda to make Ruby feel old. Ruby sighed. She only got like this when she hadn't gotten enough sleep, and by the looks of this case, that deficit wasn't going to be brought back into black for a while.

"Took you long enough, Hunter. I am starving!"

Gabe reached out for the bag before Ruby even had the chance to sit down.

"Did you happen to find anything while I was gone?"

"Nothing, which seems to be a trend with this case. Here are the pages you asked to be printed."

Gabe handed over a stack of paper that was almost half an inch thick. He patted the chair she had been sitting in earlier, beckoning her to sit down. Then, he pulled out the food, placing one black, oblong container in front of the empty chair and another in front of himself.

"Let's eat," he smiled. Ruby sat down as he handed her cutlery rolled up in a napkin. "I ordered you the same thing I got but with a lime tomatillo sauce. Lots of flavor but very little spice."

Ruby wasn't sure if it was how Gabe was raised or just who he was but gathering around food seemed important to him. It was such a foreign concept to her. Growing up, Ruby ate whatever she could find in the house and usually it was before her parents got home or after they went to sleep. Maybe that was why she hadn't put a lot of focus on going out and doing things with Asher. Well, that and their relationship was technically not appropriate by HR's standards.

Ruby watched Gabe smell the food as he pulled the lid off. He looked like he'd died and gone to heaven. Ruby hesitated. She wasn't sure her bland palate was capable of appreciating what appeared to be the food of the gods based on Gabe's reaction.

"Don't let it get cold, Ruby."

Ruby pulled the lid off her container and was immediately hit with the aroma of freshly squeezed limes, the clean scent of cilantro, and the earthy smell of pinto beans. It looked and smelled as delectable as Gabe had said.

The burrito was overstuffed and as large as Ruby's face. She watched Gabe use a fork and knife to cut his, so she did the same. Normally, she'd pick it up but it was covered in too much gooey cheese and sauce to do so. The first bite was every bit as scrumptious as it'd looked. Once she started eating, she wasn't sure she was going to stop. All she knew was this was one of the best burritos she had ever had in her life.

Ruby could only eat about half of the burrito. When she was full, she put the lid back on the container.

"Done already?" Gabe asked as he stuck a forkful of the burrito into his mouth.

"Yeah. I am stuffed."

"Did you like it?"

"Yeah. Thank you for the recommendation."

"I don't know, Ruby, you don't sound all that enthusiastic to me."

"Gabe ..."

"Okay, here's the real question: would you eat it again?" Gabe smiled, eating another chunk of his food. She rolled her eyes and then, just for effect, nodded as dramatically as she could muster. "Now that I know you have good taste, you can order our food next time."

Ruby grabbed the container and started off in the direction of the kitchenette. There was a refrigerator in there she could leave it in until she either headed home, or it was time to eat again.

"I'll take that," Gabe called after her.

"You have your own."

"Yes, but if you put that in the office fridge, you'll never see it again. I have a cooler under my desk. Hand it here."

Ruby laughed. Maybe he'd been a Boy Scout as a child, since he always seemed prepared. She handed over the container as she sat down in the chair next to Gabe. Then she started going through the numbers on the first page of information he'd given her.

Three pages in, Ruby noticed three calls to the same number with a Maryland area code. She highlighted them. On page ten, she discovered three calls to the same number with an Ohio area code.

"Hey, I might have something. Can you look up this number? It's 330-434-3134."

"It's the Akron BMV."

"*D*MV?" she asked, emphasizing the letter "d" to confirm if she'd misheard him.

"No, *B*MV. Bureau of Motor Vehicles."

"Hmmm. Okay. What about 410-768-7000?"

"It's the MVA Salisbury branch. 'MVA' stands for Motor Vehicle Administration in case you didn't know."

"Huh."

"Huh what?" Gabe asked with a furrowed brow.

"Fernanda Torres made multiple calls to the Akron BMV just days before Daisy Hauser was murdered. She has the same pattern of calls to the MVA just prior to Averie Phelps's homicide. I think the killer was getting whatever he needed to select his victims through the DMV, or whatever they call it locally."

"But Fernanda Torres wasn't home. We already confirmed she was in New York."

"Then he was using her phone. Maybe they are all working together, like a network or something. Could you print out the most recent list of calls?"

"Sure, but if they're working together, then is Fernanda Torres an accessory to murder?"

"Possibly. Although, based on what we saw with the other two cases, they might have some sort of protocol in place so there's plausible deniability."

"Do you think she knows who it is?"

"In my gut? Yes. Can I prove it? Probably not."

Gabe clicked his mouse a few times and then got up, heading toward the printer. Ruby opened her laptop and pulled up her email. She quickly filled out an InfoQuest ticket for the Tech Ops team. They needed a list of both current employees and any who might've transferred, quit, or been fired from the Akron, Ohio, Bureau of Motor Vehicles and the Salisbury, Maryland, Motor Vehicles Administration branch. Ruby marked the ticket as "urgent" and hit send. Hopefully, it wouldn't take too long to get the information they needed to find their killer.

CHAPTER TWENTY

The man smiled as he drove past the *Welcome to West Virginia* sign.

One state down, four more to go.

He could have driven the twelve-hour route in one day, but he wanted to savor every moment of the hunt. He also wanted to be sure he was well-rested and in top form. Otherwise, he was leaving too much room for error.

His phone buzzed on the dash, grabbing his attention. The man swiped his pattern lock for the secure folder. Then he tapped on the Reddit app and checked the message. It was from @LadyoftheValley13. He tapped to have it read aloud so he could stay focused on driving.

"Proverbs 14:23. The Lord is gracious, Bartholomew. The path is clear."

The man smiled at the good news. Then he tapped the record button to respond.

"Nos sumus stellae beatorum Ad astra." He tapped the record button to stop recording and hit send.

We are the stars of the blessed indeed, he thought to himself as he signed off with their standard "to the star" protocol.

His excitement soared now that Fernanda had confirmed, without a doubt, that Ruby Hunter and the FBI weren't anywhere close to catching him.

The man reached over to the thirteen-threaded rope coiled in his passenger set and pulled one end toward him. He kept his eyes on the road as he rolled the rope between his fingers, counting each strand he'd woven into it. He did this over and over, a silent prayer for the offering he was preparing to make.

One of the things the professor had taught him was to take his time and have patience. He'd spent years waiting for his chance to prove his loyalty and devotion. Then, with one phone call from Fernanda, he'd been "activated."

The professor had taught them all how to be the best version of themselves, how important it was to wait for their calling. The man had done just that, and he'd probably waited the longest for his moment in the light.

Fernanda had assured him the other two that had come before him were just trial runs. The professor was testing the FBI, and in particular Special Agent Ruby Hunter. He wanted to see them scramble, to always be too late to the scene.

Once the professor helped the man get clean, they'd become close, brothers in arms so-to-speak. But really, the professor had continued to teach the man how fragile life was and the importance of living up to his true potential. He'd met some of the others, but none of them were like him. The professor hadn't spent the same amount of time with them as he had with the man, and most of them knew it.

He was the favored one, the one who was going to ensure the professor would have his moment in the light again. The man relished the idea of being the one to free the professor from the bonds of civility. He didn't belong in a cage. He was evolution in action, no longer a man and no longer someone to be contained.

The man's sense of excitement started to build. It was only a matter of time until they would all be together again, and everyone would see how special he was just like the professor did. The thought thrilled him to no end. And if Special Agent Ruby Hunter got in his way, he'd make sure her light was snuffed out once and for all.

CHAPTER TWENTY ONE

Every time they got even a step ahead, it was like the universe knocked them back ten feet. Ruby was so fed up with Vallejo and his sickos. Something had to give.

Once Ruby and Gabe got the four-page list of BMV employees from Tech Ops, they each took two pages and started cross-referencing them. Ruby compared each name on the BMV to the MVA and ran background checks on any matches. So far, she hadn't found anything.

She continued to check her list, frustrated that it was the only lead they had. She wasn't sure how much time they had left until the killer struck again, or even if he would. They still hadn't identified the pattern the killer was following, how he was selecting his victims, or anything else that would help them stop another murder in time. It felt like they had been dumped in the middle of the ocean and told to swim toward shore, only there was no shore in sight, and they had no way to tell which way to go.

You're running out of time, Special Agent Hunter.

Fernanda Torres's words of warning rang in Ruby's head like alarm bells. She feared that Fernanda was right, and she wouldn't be able to save this one. Ruby wasn't sure she could take telling another family how sorry she was for their loss. She looked over at Gabe. He definitely wasn't up for another victim.

All she could do right now was search the list of names in front of her and take each task one step at a time. Hopefully, something would turn up.

"I might have something, Hunter."

Ruby looked up.

"There was a transfer from the Salisbury MVA to the Akron BMV four weeks ago. That would have been right around the time of Daisy Hauser's murder."

Ruby watched as Gabe typed the name "Chad Richardson" into their records search. The loading bar seemed to be taking forever, which only made her more antsy for the results. It took almost a full minute before a "No Records Found" box popped up. Gabe opened a different window and typed in the man's name. In less than ten seconds, a box popped up showing "1 record found."

"He's got a juvie record."

"I'll pull up his driver's license. Let's see if he matches the physical description before we have to go running down a judge to unseal his records."

"I might have a work-around. Let me make a quick call," Gabe said as he got up and left with his cell phone.

Ruby was curious who Gabe was reaching out to, but she figured maybe it was better she didn't know. She knew he had military connections. Maybe those connections included people in Intelligence or Cyber Crime. At the end of the day, all that mattered to Ruby is that they got to the killer before he got to his next victim.

She typed "Chad Richardson" into the licensing database. Over 41,400 results came back. She then typed in the criteria for places he lived. Five seconds later, the Ohio license for Chadwick Kevin Richardson was on Ruby's screen. She studied his face for a moment, estimating he was in his late twenties, maybe early thirties. He had curly, brown hair that looked like it needed to be cut and brown eyes with dark circles underneath. He sneered at the camera, like he was annoyed he'd had to have his picture taken.

Ruby looked at the rest of the license. He was twenty-nine, six-foot-three, and just over 200 pounds. He checked every box of their unsub.

When Gabe returned a few minutes later and sat down, Ruby showed him her screen with Chadwick Richardson's face.

"He fits the physical profile."

"My contact said his record was sealed because he was arrested at fifteen for stalking, but they had to let him go. They didn't have any proof he'd done anything wrong."

"Another stalker. That can't be a coincidence. Right?"

"Honestly? I have no idea anymore, Ruby."

Ruby sighed. She wasn't sure about anything anymore either. Gabe picked up the receiver on his desk phone and dialed a number.

"Who are you calling?"

"The Akron BMV. Might as well find out if he's there before we fly all the way back."

"Good thinking."

Ruby pulled up everything she could about Chadwick Kevin Richardson online and through social media. Most of the pictures on his social media were of rivers, trees, and night photography. Ruby stopped on one picture that looked oddly familiar.

Orion's Lookout.

She tapped her screen to get Gabe's attention. His eyes widened, and he nodded. She continued looking through Chadwick Richardson's life, hoping to find another clue. As she did, she listened to Gabe talk with someone at the Akron BMV.

"I completely understand. I am putting in the paperwork as we speak and will have it forwarded to your manager. While I am doing that, would you please do me a favor? Google the phone number I am calling you from. It'll show you I am calling you from Quantico, Virginia. You can even look up my information, and it'll show my place of employment is the Federal Bureau of Investigation. Gabriel Mestas Ruiz."

Ruby had to give Gabe credit. He knew how to turn on the charm to get what he wanted. She wasn't one to cut corners but skirting around the edges didn't hurt anything. Especially when they were running out of time.

Gabe hung up the phone and started typing on his computer.

"What did you find out?"

"Chadwick Richardson took PTO this week to go visit his mother in Bohicket, Florida, which is just south of Tampa. I am checking our flight options, which aren't looking so great."

"Bellisario can get us a charter flight."

Ruby got up from her desk and walked over to Bellisario's office. He was busy writing something and didn't notice her standing in the doorway. He was always busy. She was certain that's why he was so good at his job. He never rested on his laurels or waited for other people to do the work like Murphy did.

Ruby knocked on the doorframe.

"Special Agent Hunter. Come in."

Ruby walked in and sat down.

"Do you have a lead?"

"We do. In Florida. He fits the physical profile and has a potential history of stalking."

"You got anything else that ties him to any of the victims?"

"He moved from Salisbury, Maryland, to Akron, Ohio, shortly after Averie Phelps's murder. And he works for the DMV, which gives him access to whatever criteria he needs to select his next victim."

"What do you need from me?"

Ruby appreciated how Bellisario always knew how to get to the guts of the situation quickly.

"We checked for flights to Tampa, and there isn't anything until late tomorrow morning. We need a charter. This guy is ahead of us, and we need all the time we can get."

He let out a sigh.

She didn't understand his hesitation. "Sir?"

He put his hand on his phone receiver. "You've got to be sure about this. Murphy wants to put certain limits on your activities."

Her mouth fell open. No, she wasn't sure. But what Murphy wanted to do was hinder her, whether or not people ended up dead because of it. She'd be blamed, no matter what. She knew that. "I'm sure."

"All right." He picked up the phone.

Ruby briskly walked back over to Gabe and started grabbing her things.

"We're going to the airport," she said as she headed toward the elevator. Gabe fell into step behind her as the doors slid open.

"That was fast."

"Guess it's good to be king," Ruby smiled.

Forty minutes later, they pulled into a private parking lot at the airport. They checked in and were directed to a secure waiting area near the gate. Ruby plugged in her phone and laptop so they would be fully charged for the flight. Gabe did the same.

The gate agent let them know they were locating a flight crew. He said he'd check back with them once he had some news or it was time to leave.

"I am really tired of airports."

"Yeah ... it's too bad we aren't earning any air miles. We could probably take one heck of a vacation if we were."

Ruby agreed. They may not be earning points or miles or whatever, but that didn't mean they had to keep going from case to case without a break. Maybe once they solved this case, they could both take some time off. Ruby wasn't sure where she would go or what she would do, but the idea of unplugging from the world sounded very appealing.

Maybe she'd go stay in one of those cabins in the mountains of the Pacific Northwest where there was no cell signal and get lost for a few days. She wasn't sure why, but she definitely liked the possibility of it. She made a mental note to ask Gabe about the best places to go in the Pacific Northwest.

Maybe there was somewhere specific he could recommend that would be remote but not completely off the grid.

When this case was over.

Which was something she didn't see happening anytime soon. It was time to fly to Florida.

CHAPTER TWENTY TWO

It was well after midnight by the time Ruby and Gabe's flight took off. At least they would get to Tampa before sunrise. Then it was at least an hour drive to Bohicket. Hopefully, Chadwick Richardson was still there.

The cabin lights were dim, but Gabe and Ruby were both wide awake. She looked out the window at the stars. She could not see the moon from where she was sitting, but she didn't mind. The stars were beautiful.

"Do you think the thing with the stars was just another red herring?"

Ruby shrugged. "I suppose we won't know until we do."

"Isn't that true about everything?"

Ruby smirked. "Probably. I am just tired of trying to out-think this guy. I could not do it with Vallejo, and so far, I am not having much luck on this case either."

"What do you mean? You caught Vallejo."

"Vallejo *let* me catch him. The only thing he didn't know was if I was going to do the honorable thing and arrest him, or if I was going to put a bullet between his eyes. He had a 50/50 chance of either."

"I doubt that. Aside from a few folks in the desert, you're one of the most honorable people I know."

Ruby knew Gabe's compliment was not a comment to be taken lightly. She also knew Gabe Ruiz had vastly misjudged her.

"Thank you, but I can honestly say I don't know if I would have done the same thing back then if I'd known how things were going to end up. Taking Vallejo out might've ended my career and maybe put me behind bars, but there's also a good chance the nine women in these last three cases would still be alive."

"Ruby, that's not how it works. We have no idea when he started recruiting these people. If you'd put him down back then and he'd already gotten to these people, we'd be completely lost. There's a good possibility that in that timeline more than nine women are dead. At least, for now, we can get some semblance of information from him even if it's riddles wrapped in nonsense."

Ruby considered Gabe's point. It's true if Vallejo had started recruiting his followers before he was caught, it wouldn't necessarily change how things had been recently. Or it might've changed things for the worse because she wouldn't have Vallejo to consult.

"That's fair," she conceded with a half-smile.

"Do you mind if I ask you a question about something?"

"Sure, what do you want to know?"

"Was it true what you told Fernanda Torres earlier? About you and Special Agent Carnes?"

Ruby wasn't sure how to respond. She'd known he was listening, and she'd known he might have questions. She just hadn't thought through how to handle those questions.

Gabe immediately took her silence for intrusion.

"You don't have to answer that if you don't want. I was just wondering. 'Being nosy' as my mom would say."

"It's fine, really. Yes, it was true. I was with Asher the night Vallejo killed him. We'd agreed to tell Bellisario the next day that we were dating. You know, make it official. After he died, no one asked questions. We were partners. That's what people saw."

"Do you think that's why Vallejo killed Asher? Because he's fixated on you?"

"Before recently, I hadn't given it much thought. I told Fernanda that to make her jealous, hoping it would trip her up. But I have no idea if that's the case. I honestly can't read him to even guess what his feelings for me might be. It's never clear when I'm there in front of him, or I'm too distracted by my history with him to notice. I know he likes playing games with people. Maybe that's a game he played with her."

"Maybe."

"How much do you know about Special Agent Carnes's death?"

"I read the case files."

Ruby raised her eyebrows in surprise. "You did?"

"Yeah. I knew you had this complicated history with Vallejo, so I figured I should do whatever I could to know as much as possible without having been there. I didn't want to have to ask you to relive it if I didn't have to. It didn't seem fair to do that to you."

His words and the thought of Gabe going out of his way to learn the history she'd lived comforted her. It was a foreign feeling, something she hadn't felt since before Asher's death, but it wasn't a bad thing.

She'd just forgotten what it was like to have someone be considerate of her or her feelings in a long time.

"I appreciate you taking the time to do that, Gabe. I can't imagine it was easy to read about what he did to his victims."

"I can't imagine it was easy living through it."

"No, it wasn't. And I'll deny it if you ever tell anyone I said this, but I still have nightmares about some of the things I saw. It just never goes away, not when it's that bad."

"I know you want to protect me, Ruby. That's why I read those files. So, I could have some idea of the hell you went through, why you shut me out all the time. But I am your partner. And I have to trust that you have my back just as much as I have yours. You don't have to keep protecting me. In fact, I'd prefer it if you didn't. Okay?"

Ruby wasn't sure how she should or wanted to respond. What he was asking seemed simple enough, but Ruby knew it was anything but. Instead of trying to come up with the right thing to say, she just nodded.

"It's been a long couple of days."

"Yes, it has. We still have a while before we land. I am going to close my eyes for a little while. Maybe the answers will come to me in a dream."

"Maybe so," Gabe agreed. He leaned his seat back and closed his eyes. Ruby was jealous it seemed to take so little effort for him to fall asleep. She had no doubt it was a skill he'd acquired through years of strenuous circumstances and training that she was grateful she hadn't had to go through. He just made it look so easy. It was easy to envy how simple he made complicated things seem.

Ruby realized that before that moment, no one else besides her and Asher had really known all the gory details of the Lucky 13 murders. Even the jury got a watered-down version. It was what was best for everyone. Part of her wanted to talk to Gabe about the murders, get his perspective as someone who wasn't there but had studied the case files.

She wasn't sure that was something he'd be open to, but maybe they could talk about it sometime after this case was solved. Then again, maybe it was better to not talk about all the horror she'd seen. It might bring it all rushing back to the surface, and she wasn't sure she was ready to deal with everything she'd been through thanks to Vincent Vallejo.

Ruby unfolded the blanket the flight attendant had given her earlier and turned on the air vent. She sat down, thinking of what Bellisario had said. *Are you sure?*

No, she wasn't sure about anything. And more than ever, her neck was on the line. But Murphy was just a bully. If it cost her her job . . . it would be worth it. She couldn't stand to think that another person might die on her watch.

But if this lead didn't work out, she was lost.

Dread pooled her gut at the thought.

Her phone buzzed. She pulled it out of her pocket and checked what it was.

The notification showed she'd gotten an email. She swiped open the app and saw her old mentor, Carl Rivers, had sent her a message.

Hi Ruby,

We haven't spoken in a while, and I know we'll connect when there's time. I just wanted to touch base and say hello. I have been watching the news, so I know they're keeping you busy. I know you might not be able to get together anytime soon, so I figured I'd just send you a quick note.

I was going through some old boxes in the garage, and I came across one of the papers you'd written for my class. You got an A- because of spelling errors, but it was exceptional. It was an analysis on the public's perception of Ted Bundy and John Wayne Gacy and how skewed it was. To this day, it's probably still one of the best papers I have ever read.

Anyway, I won't keep you. I just wanted to share that with you and hopefully remind you that your light is so much brighter than their darkness.

Carl

Ruby struggled not to let the tears fall as she locked her phone and put it back in her pocket. She didn't know how, but Carl Rivers always seemed to know exactly what to say and when to say it. It was his little reminders like this email that had kept her going when she was chasing Vallejo. Somehow, just when she'd forgotten she was on the side of right, he stepped back into her life and jogged her memory.

Carl Rivers had been her Psychology of Criminal Behavior professor in college. He was in his late forties, divorced, and had been a consultant for the FBI for four years. His silvering hair had a slight wave to it, and he always looked like he needed to shave. 'Ruggedly handsome' is the phrase Ruby heard people use most often when they described him. Ruby never really noticed.

Carl was the one who'd suggested she would do well as a profiler. At the time, Ruby was studying Criminal Justice with the intention of becoming a lawyer. She wasn't sure that's what she wanted to do, but it seemed like a good idea at the time, especially because the money was good.

He'd asked her to come by during office hours to discuss a paper she'd turned in, which she immediately took as a bad sign. She still remembered how nervous she was when she knocked on the white, wooden door. He quickly put her at ease and told her she'd gotten high marks. He explained he just wanted some insight as to why she'd picked the topic and to learn more about the research she'd done.

They spent the next three hours talking about serial killers, conspiracy theories, and everything in between. It was one of the best conversations she had ever had. He encouraged her to look into the FBI, and more specifically the BAU. He believed her perception of serial killers was spot on, and her ability to analyze their behavior was better than anyone he'd met who actually worked at the FBI.

He'd been her mentor ever since, which was especially helpful during the Vallejo case. Ruby remembered when Carl and Asher met. It was the first time she had ever seen Asher get jealous. Ruby tried to reassure him, but Asher could see how much she respected Carl and how much he'd supported her career. He thought that maybe they'd had something more, but Carl was the one who stepped in and cleared the air. They had never had anything outside the classroom except a mentor-mentee relationship, and they never would. That was also the first and only time Ruby had seen Asher feel embarrassed.

After Asher's death, Carl had checked in on her every couple of days. He'd call, send emails, and even come by if he hadn't heard from her. He and Jocelyn were the only ones who kept her from drowning in grief. Ruby had no idea what she would've done without them.

Before she returned to the FBI, she usually talked to him at least twice a month. Lately that hadn't been possible with the cases they'd been working. Ruby felt bad that she was slacking in reaching out, something she made a mental note to correct as soon as they solved this case.

CHAPTER TWENTY THREE

The Tampa field office was not much different than Headquarters, just smaller with more windows. Ruby and Gabe coordinated with the local office to locate Chadwick Richardson. His mother lived in Bohicket, but that didn't mean that's where Chadwick was.

Ruby caught a reflection of the two of them in the elevator and harrumphed. They both looked ridiculously tired. Like zombie apocalypse tired. Hopefully, they still looked somewhat professional.

"What was that for?" Gabe asked when his puzzled look didn't solicit an explanation.

"We look as tired as we feel." She nodded at their reflection. He followed her gesture and smirked.

"There's only so much we can do with the schedule we're keeping. At least we don't smell."

Ruby giggled. The local agent with them gave them a judgmental look as the elevator door slid open. Her bleached blonde hair was pulled back into a severe bun, and her face looked perpetually pinched. Ruby wondered if the woman looked like that all the time or just when she had to do something she thought was beneath her.

"We have two desks right there you can use, and I'll get Milo from Tech Ops online for you." The woman walked away without another word.

"And I thought you were stiff," Gabe half-whispered as he leaned over to Ruby.

"No, I am *guarded. She's* stiff. There is a difference, you know."

A few minutes later, Gabe and Ruby were video chatting with Milo. He was running a system analysis to triangulate Chadwick Richardson's cell phone signal.

"I desperately need some coffee if we're going to have to drive out to Bohicket. Do you want any?" Gabe asked.

"Yes, please. The biggest cup you can find."

"Okay, I'll be back in a few."

Ruby nodded and focused back on Milo. He had large, blue eyes, thin lips, and a strong, square jaw. He looked like someone you'd see dropping his kids off at school or cheering them on in the stands. He spoke faster than Ruby could type, and he had an answer for everything.

It took a minute, probably because Ruby was so exhausted, but she realized she knew who Milo was. According to Asher, Milo Quincy was somewhat of a legend. Quantico had been trying to get him to transfer from Tampa almost since the day he joined the FBI. A self-taught hacker who'd toed the line between black and white hat hacking, he was known in the hacker community as "Lil Mitnick," a reference to his height and the infamous 1980s hacker, Kevin Mitnick.

"I am glad you're the one helping us, Milo," Ruby smiled.

"Oh yeah? Why is that?" he asked as he continued pounding away at the keyboard offscreen.

"Did you ever meet Special Agent Carnes? Asher Carnes?"

Milo's face lit up and then dimmed immediately. It was often the expression people had when Asher's name was mentioned since his murder. Joy, then remembering, then sadness all in a matter of seconds. Ruby knew that emotional rollercoaster all too well.

"He was a great agent, but I liked him more as a man."

"Same. He always told me you were the best, so I am glad we get to work with you."

"Actually, he was one of the reasons I seriously considered moving to Virginia," Milo offered while he continued working. Ruby also knew what he wasn't saying. Asher's death was probably the same reason he decided *against* moving to Virginia.

"All right, it looks like your unsub is at the address I just sent to your phone. It's not Mr. Richardson's mother's house, though. It looks like someone named Victoria Daniels lives there."

Ruby thought to herself, *this could be it. This could be their guy.*

"Thank you, Milo. Please come visit us at Quantico any time. Our servers are better than yours, you know," Ruby smiled. Milo grinned from ear-to-ear, but his eyes didn't fill with the joy the rest of his face held. Ruby knew why, though. It was a saying she'd heard Asher say to him every time they spoke. He was the one person Asher trusted to find information on people when he needed it fast.

"Don't be a stranger, Special Agent Hunter."

Gabe walked up with two large cups of coffee just as Milo waved goodbye.

"How long was I gone?" Gabe asked, handing over Ruby's coffee.

"Don't worry. Milo's just that fast. Turns out Chadwick Richardson is not at his mother's house, but instead at Victoria Daniels's house, which is only about ten minutes from here. I just forwarded the address to your phone."

"Then we better get going."

Ruby hurried behind Gabe as they headed to the elevators. He walked with purpose, seeming to have found a second wind on his way to get coffee. Unfortunately, Ruby could not say the same.

"Was that who I think it was?"

"Who? Milo?"

"Yeah, his face looked familiar so while I was waiting for the coffee, I googled him. He's *that* Milo?"

"The one and only."

"That's so cool."

"Wow, Gabe, I don't think I have ever seen this side of you before."

"And what side is that, Ruby?" he asked as they stepped off the elevator and headed toward the doors.

"The fanboy side," she laughed, unable to resist the opportunity to tease him like he'd teased her. He chuckled and shook his head at her like he couldn't believe she'd gone there.

A minute later, they pulled out of the parking lot and followed the directions on the GPS. It was early enough that there wasn't any traffic yet, so they made it to Victoria Daniels's house in less than eight minutes.

Gabe turned off the engine and rubbed his face as if he was trying to make himself more alert. As they stepped out of the vehicle, they heard a woman screaming so loudly that it sounded like she was about to snap her vocal cords.

Ruby's adrenaline kicked into overdrive as she and Gabe ran toward the house. Gabe reached the door first, checking the door handle to see if it was open. Just as he was about to knock and announce "FBI," they heard a loud crash and glass breaking.

They pulled their weapons as Gabe kicked in the door. "FBI!"

CHAPTER TWENTY FOUR

Ruby recognized Chadwick Richardson immediately. His curly, brown hair was matted, like he had been sweating profusely, and he was brandishing a kitchen knife. A young, dark-haired woman crouched next to a China hutch, crying and trying to shield herself from harm.

"FBI! Chadwick Richardson, drop the knife. Drop the knife, right now!" Ruby yelled. Chadwick Richardson looked at her, looked at Gabe, and then took off toward the back of the house. Gabe launched himself after the suspect while Ruby checked on who she assumed was Victoria Daniels.

"Are you Victoria Daniels? Did he hurt you?"

"Yes, that's me. I don't know," she sobbed.

"I am going to call for backup and a medic just in case, okay? I'll be right back."

"No, please! Please don't leave!" the woman lunged at Ruby, desperate for safety. Ruby caught her and held her for a moment while she cried.

The next thing she knew, Ruby heard a car door slam and gun shots. Her heart dropped into her stomach.

"Victoria? Victoria. I need to go make sure my partner's okay. I promise I'll be right back."

Ruby gently guided the woman into the nearest chair, squeezed her arms in reassurance, and took off out the front door.

Outside, she saw a blur race past her. Gabe.

She gave chase, hearing shouts up ahead, but unable to make out the words.

Just as she rounded a corner, she stopped short before careening into his shoulder blades. He was standing with his gun pointed at Chadwick Richardson, who was zip tied and lying face down on the ground. Relief washed over her when she saw that Gabe hadn't been shot.

They made eye contact, and she nodded at him as if to say, "good work." They were peers, after all, so it wasn't really her place to actually say it out loud. Ruby took a moment to catch her breath and assess the scene.

She quickly realized that Chadwick Richardson must've tried to escape, and Gabe had shot out the front tire. The man lost control of the vehicle and wound up banging into a tree. She noticed the red knot on Richardson's forehead and looked at Gabe.

"Steering wheel," he shrugged.

Ruby nodded. "Did you call for backup already?"

"Yeah, and a medic too. Just in case."

"You good?" she double-checked. He looked fine, but she needed to hear him say it. That was something she and Asher had always done, verbally check-in after a chase or high-pressure situation. Ruby had thought at the time that it was because they were also involved, but now she knew it was more a partner thing than a lover thing.

"Yep."

Ruby wondered for a second if Gabe was the reason Chadwick Richardson had the welp on his forehead. If he was, Chadwick wasn't saying anything about it, so she wasn't going to ask.

Ruby went back inside and checked on Victoria. She had her arms wrapped around her tightly, as if she was cold, but Ruby knew it was shock.

"Victoria, are you hurt?"

The young woman shook her head and sniffled.

Ruby walked into the kitchen and saw a broken bottle of red wine all over the floor. That must've been the breaking glass they had heard. She moved back to the hallway and headed toward the back of the house. The backdoor was deadbolted, so she wondered how did Chadwick Richardson, and Gabe for that matter, end up outside.

To the right was a half bathroom and to the left was a large bedroom. Ruby walked into the large room and discovered where Chadwick Richardson had made his exit. The back wall of the room was mostly taken up by sliding glass doors, which led onto a screen porch. The doors were wide open.

Ruby walked through and saw the screen porch door was off its hinges, lying in the yard. Everything else seemed to be intact.

Ruby returned to Victoria to make sure she was doing okay. She heard the police sirens getting closer, which made Ruby feel better.

"The police will be here any minute along with a medic to make sure you're okay. My partner has Mr. Richardson in custody, so you're safe now, okay?"

"I can't believe this is happening," she sobbed.

Ruby sat down across from Victoria and patted her knee. The young woman wiped her face on her sleeve and tried to calm down, which only made her more upset.

"Try taking some slow, deep breaths for me. Is there anyone we need to call?"

Victoria shook her head. She shuddered as she sucked in air, whimpering from trying to stifle her tears. Ruby took a long, slow breath, encouraging Victoria to do the same. They did that a few times until Victoria finally calmed down enough to talk.

"Can you tell me what happened?"

She sniffled and then nodded. "We met online a couple of months ago. We were both chatting on the same livestream, and he was telling all of these hilarious dad jokes. We hit it off and started chatting just one-on-one. He seemed really nice, like everything a girl could ask for in a partner. We talked every day, sometimes multiple times a day, and it was just really nice to have someone to talk to about stuff. I wasn't in a rush to get into another relationship, which I told him up front. The last guy I dated cheated on me, so I just wanted to take things slow. He said he understood, and that that's what he'd wanted too."

"What changed?"

"He started talking about getting together, meeting up in real life. But I kept telling him I wasn't ready. He'd let it go, and then a week or so later, he'd start back up again asking to meet up. Then he started texting me when I was out with my friends and accusing me of seeing other guys. It was just too much. I told him I couldn't handle the drama, that I needed a break, but he wouldn't let up. Finally, three days ago, I decided I just couldn't take it anymore. I texted him that we were over and stopped responding to him. I blocked him on everything—social media, my phone, everything. It seemed like the best thing to do at the time."

"When did he show up here?"

"About five minutes before y'all showed up. He started banging on my door, and I was worried it was someone who was hurt or something. The door doesn't have a peep hole, so I opened it just a little bit to see who was outside. When I saw it was Chad, I immediately tried to shut the door, but he pushed his way in."

"Did he have the knife with him?"

"No. I ran to the kitchen and grabbed the knife to defend myself. He knocked it out of my hand, so I grabbed the closest thing to me, a bottle of wine, and threw it at him. Then, he picked up the knife like he was going to stab me with it. That's when you came in."

"It sounds like you did a pretty good job defending yourself, Victoria."

"I don't know about that. I tried, I guess. You can call me Tori."

"All right, Tori. Our backup just got here, so I am going to walk with you outside. We need to get you checked out, and you'll need to give your statement to the local police. Okay?"

"Okay ... what's going to happen to Chad?"

"Well, he's going to come with my partner and me down to the station so he can answer some questions for us. Then, depending on how he answers our questions, it may be up to you and the local authorities to press charges."

"I just think he needs some help, you know? For like mental health stuff. I don't know if he needs to go to *jail*," Tori reasoned. Ruby wondered if the change in her tone was fueled by guilt or because she really cared about him.

"I'm sure we'll get to the bottom of it. Okay?"

"Yeah," Tori said with a deep sigh.

Ruby walked the young woman outside and steered her to a female officer. She told the officer briefly who Tori was and what had happened. The officer immediately took over and led Tori to the ambulance.

Gabe guarded Chadwick Richardson's head as he put him in the back of a black-and-white. Ruby caught his attention and forced the best tight-lipped smile she could. He nodded his head toward their vehicle, indicating he was ready to go.

A minute later, Ruby and Gabe were on their way back to the Tampa field office to interview Chadwick Richardson for the murders of Fran McCormick, Averie Phelps, and Daisy Hauser.

CHAPTER TWENTY FIVE

"I'll take this one," Ruby said as they stepped off the elevator.

"That's probably for the best," Gabe agreed. Suspects didn't like to be caught, much less zip tied. Ruby knew Chadwick Richardson was likely to be on the defensive with Gabe, and that wouldn't help them get the answers they needed.

They were both dead on their feet, but hopefully they had finally reached the finish line. Gabe followed Ruby to the secure interview room where Chadwick Richardson was being held.

"I'll double tap the table if I need you in there, okay?"

Gabe nodded and handed Ruby the files for the three murders they were investigating. Then, with a smile of encouragement, he walked into the office just outside the interview room. Four cameras were set up in each room to ensure all interviews were above board. The camera feed was viewable in the office so multiple people could watch what was going on. This was not unusual, especially if the field office had interns or hosted training classes from the Academy.

Ruby opened the door to the interview room and sat down across from Chadwick Kevin Richardson. She placed the files on the table in a neat pile before gauging Richardson's willingness to cooperate. He had a bandage wrapped around the top of his head and some scratches on his arms. His hands were handcuffed to the table, and his feet were shackled to the chair. Ruby wondered if he'd tried to escape or was being too difficult for the guards to handle. It seemed a little excessive to have him restrained to such an extent, but then again, he was the prime suspect in three homicides.

"Hello, Mr. Richardson."

"Umm ... hi?"

"My name is Special Agent Ruby Hunter, and I am with the FBI. My partner, Special Agent Ruiz, is the one who arrested you. Are you comfortable? Can I get you anything to drink before we get started?"

"Are you serious?"

"Given the circumstances, yes. I am very serious."

"Look, this is all just a huge misunderstanding. Talk to Tori. She'll tell you I didn't do anything wrong. I just surprised her is all."

"I think you did more than surprise her, Mr. Richardson. Breaking and entering is a crime in the state of Florida last time I checked."

"Please stop calling me that. My name is Chad. And I didn't break in. Is that what she's saying? That's not what happened at all!"

"Okay, so why don't you tell me what happened, *Chad*. Then we can clear everything up."

The young man looked around with a sense of desperation like he was in a nightmare and hoping someone, anyone, was going to wake him up any minute. He clocked the cameras and then looked back at Ruby with a wide-eyed expression, like he was finally grasping the gravity of his situation. One of his legs was bobbing up and down furiously under the table, shaking the chain around his ankle.

Ruby remained silent, allowing space for the man to get uncomfortable enough to start talking. She watched him squirm in his seat, although his movements were limited. It didn't even take a full minute before he spoke up.

"Look, I don't know what Tori told you, but this is all a horrible misunderstanding."

"Okay, let's say you're telling the truth. Explain to me why you were brandishing a knife when we arrived on the scene."

"*Tori* had the knife and threatened *me* with it. I managed to knock it out of her hand, but then she threw a full bottle of wine at me. I'm *lucky* she missed. That could've done some serious damage, you know?"

"Why was she threatening you with a knife?"

"I don't know. Maybe she was just surprised to see me? I kept asking her to calm down so we could talk, but she started screaming like a mental person and wouldn't stop. I just wanted to talk. That's it. I told her that, but she grabbed the knife and started jabbing at me like she was going to kill me."

Ruby spread the files out in front of her and opened each one to reveal a crime scene photo of the victims. Fran McCormick, Averie Phelps, and Daisy Hauser.

"Did you want to *just talk* to these women too?"

Chadwick Richardson visibly cringed as he looked at the faces of the dead women. His expression transformed from confusion to horror as he realized what Ruby was really asking him.

"No, no, no, no, no. I didn't do this. This isn't me. I don't know any of these women. You've got to believe me. *I just wanted to talk to Tori*!" he sobbed, fear overwhelming him.

Ruby watched him break down, scrutinizing every move for genuine emotion. He wept as if he would never stop, breathing so hard that he began hyperventilating. This was not the reaction of a killer. This was the reaction of a scared child, who didn't know how bad they'd messed up until this very moment.

Ruby thought back to Miles Barker's sniveling nonsense, which he'd turned off like a switch. She'd believed him at first, everyone did. But then, he couldn't keep the act going. Psychopaths rarely can fake genuine emotion for long periods of time. They get their amusement more from showing others how easily they can pretend to care. She knew just by Chadwick Richardson's physiological reaction, there was no way he could suddenly stop the avalanche of emotion that had overcome him.

Ruby looked at the camera and thought about tapping the table. Maybe she was too tired to see anything other than his unleashed emotion. Instead, she decided to confirm what she already knew: Chadwick Richardson was not their guy. She pulled out the notepad she always kept in her inside jacket pocket and ripped off an empty piece of paper. She wrote the dates of the homicides and slid the paper over to the sobbing man.

"Tell me where you were on each of these dates."

He leaned over to wipe the tears from his eyes with his restricted hands, but he didn't stop crying. He was still hyperventilating, but he was also struggling to calm down. Chadwick Richardson was truly terrified.

"I was working … and …" he said between sniffles and body shudders.

"Take a slow, deep breath, Chad, and tell me where you were."

He did as he was told. It took three attempts before he was able to fully inhale and exhale without his emotions taking over. "I work every day from 8 a.m. to 5 p.m. Sometimes, I would come home and talk to Tori online. Or we would video chat, almost every night. I go to bed after midnight. You can check my phone."

There it was. Three different ways Ruby could verify Chadwick Richardson was not the killer. He was just another misdirection, and the real killer was out there preparing to strike again. For all they knew, he might've already killed his fourth victim, her body was just waiting to be found.

Ruby closed the files and gathered them back into a neat pile.

"All right, Chad. We're going to confirm your whereabouts on these dates and see where we land."

"Then what?" he asked, his voice quiet and still full of trepidation.

"Then we release you to the local authorities to figure out all this stuff with Tori."

Chad's attempt to regain his composure dissolved as tears began to roll down the sides of his face. "I swear to God I never meant to upset Tori. I only came down here to tell her face-to-face how much she means to me, how I want to spend my life making her happy. I thought that's what she wanted. I even bought a ring."

Ruby truly felt sorry for Chadwick Richardson. Sure, he was awkward and clearly had a problem with boundaries, but it didn't seem like he was malicious. Misguided, yes. Ruby wasn't naïve enough to believe he was innocent, but he didn't seem like a killer.

"I appreciate your candor, Chad."

Chadwick Richardson laid his head down on the table and quietly let the tears fall. Ruby was certain he was trying to recount every step that had led him here, to understand how he could have misjudged his relationship with Tori so much. She hoped he learned something from all this. But given the stricken look on his face as she left the room, Ruby suspected he probably hadn't.

Gabe met her in the hallway, a look of defeat overwhelming his handsome features.

"Do you think we're too late?"

CHAPTER TWENTY SIX

The man pulled his car to a stop a little more than a block away from his target's home. The blue, two-story craftsman was one of the nicer homes in the area. It looked newer too. He checked the time on his phone. It was just after 5 a.m. The sun wasn't even up yet, and neither was she.

He had over fifteen hours before he could put his rope to good use. He didn't like waiting, but he had to be patient. He already had been for almost ten years. It was the only virtue his master required of him, and it was something he'd gotten very good at with many years of practice.

The man watched as lights in the home turned on. First, the light came on in the window on the second story farthest from him. Then, other lights followed in a sequence as if someone was turning them on as they moved from the top floor to the bottom.

He wondered if she was awake. Perhaps she was getting ready for work. He reached back into the cooler behind the passenger seat and pulled out a plain ham and cheese sandwich in a Ziploc sandwich bag.

He turned the car off and settled into his seat. He slowly ate his sandwich, counting his bites and watching her house for activity. It was like his own personal drive-in theater.

Around 5:30 a.m., he noticed the lights started going out in the same order they had been turned on. Then the garage door opened with red and white taillights glowing. A silver, four-door Toyota Camry backed out far enough into the driveway to clear the garage. Then the garage door closed, likely from a remote inside the vehicle.

The Camry slowly backed out into the street, the front of the car facing away from the man. A moment later, they were gone.

He sealed the empty Ziploc bag and put it in his glove box. He had more sandwiches in the cooler, but he wasn't really hungry. He wasn't sure what he was feeling.

Antsy. Ready to put his hands to work. Maybe he was bored. He needed something to distract him or else he'd never make it to midnight.

He could go fill up his gas tank, but that wouldn't take much time. He could drive around the area, get familiar with his surroundings. That wasn't a bad idea, but it gave him the inkling of something better. The man had everything he needed for later to break into the woman's home. Why wait in his car and break in after dark when he could do it now? That way he'd be ready for her once she got home, and he could truly take his time. Maybe he could plan something a little extra for this one, a true homage to his master.

The man knew it was important he didn't rush his work. He watched the street for any activity for almost an hour before stepping out of his vehicle. The last thing he wanted was to risk someone seeing him and being nosy. He had one target, and he couldn't touch her until well after the sun went down. If someone else interfered, it could ruin everything he'd worked for, everything he'd built to prove he was ready. That it was his time to shine.

The woman's street was quiet. There were no school buses driving through or kids running to a bus stop. He thought it was odd he hadn't even seen any early morning joggers. He wondered if that was more of an evening activity for the folks in the area. If so, it was a good thing his rope snatched their screams before anyone else could hear them. That part was almost his favorite, but it couldn't quite top the seeing the light dim and then go out.

The two-story home was the last home on the street, and it was surrounded by dense woods on two sides. It looked like there might be a walking trail on the left side, which would work to his advantage.

He took his time as he walked toward the trail. He was eager to get inside her home, see where and how she lived. But he didn't want his sense of urgency to draw attention. He took slow, deep breaths, allowing the serenity he'd taken years to learn wash over him. Now was not the time to hurry.

As he stepped onto the walking trail, he noticed a gate in the fencing at the back left corner of the lot. The six-foot privacy fence would hide him from view, giving him the chance to take his time.

He paced himself as he walked toward the gate, careful not to be too quick. He tried the latch. It was unlocked. He was always amazed at how lax people were with their security. The man slipped inside the gate and quietly closed it. He leaned against the fence and waited to see if anyone saw him.

Once he knew he was in the clear, the man looked around the large backyard. It had two large, oak trees and several flower beds. The grass needed cutting. Maybe she had a lawn service that did that for her.

Maybe she did it herself. He had time and was curious enough that he made a mental note to check her garage for a lawn mower.

He moved quietly along the fence until he reached the door to the screen porch. It was also unlocked. The man thought it was astonishing a single woman with no children or roommates would leave herself so exposed. It was almost like she was waiting for someone like him to come along.

The screen porch was nice with two white, wicker chairs and a matching wicker couch. There were potted plants everywhere. He kept near the back wall of the house and moved slowly toward the sliding glass door. Thankfully, the home was the same in person as it had been on its Zillow listing from a year ago when she bought it.

He leaned against the outside wall and listened for any noise from inside the home. After several minutes of silence, he decided it was time to go inside. The man pulled a screwdriver out of his back pocket—the only tool he depended on besides his rope. He wedged it at the bottom of the sliding glass door and placed his hand on the handle. Then he shoved the screwdriver into the track and, at the same time, yanked back on the door. It instantly popped the lock, and the door slid back.

The man didn't enter right away. He wanted to make sure she didn't have an alarm. He'd done his homework, but he preferred to be extra cautious. Otherwise, he would have gotten caught after he killed Fran McCormick.

He waited a good ten minutes before entering the woman's home. Once he did, he knew this was going to be his best yet. He figured that was the way he was supposed to feel, as if every time was better than the one before it. The professor had prepared him for many aspects of this journey, but he never could've prepared him for how good it felt and how much he wanted to feel that way all the time, like a drug.

CHAPTER TWENTY SEVEN

Ruby sat at her desk, reading every note she'd taken and going over the files, trying to understand what she'd missed. She had each file open, side-by-side. There had to be a connection. This killer was not just picking women's names out of a hat. There was something they weren't seeing.

Ruby looked over at Gabe. He was doing the same thing. Maybe he would find something she hadn't. Maybe they were too late. Ruby scolded herself for her fatalistic thinking. They had what they needed to solve this case. She honestly believed it. They just had to figure it out.

She focused back on her notes, hoping something would finally stand out.

Ruby started with Fran McCormick's file. She reviewed every single piece of information they had on the woman. Next, she looked at Averie Phelps's file and did the same. Still, nothing jumped out at her. Then she reread Daisy Hauser's file. All three women had nothing in common except the killer.

She went back to Fran's file. There *had* to be something. She looked through the paperwork, the requests they had put in for information, anything that might help. She compared everything she had in Fran McCormick's file to what they had in Averie Phelps's file. As she flipped the pages over, she came to Fernanda Torres's phone records that showed someone had called the MVA in Salisbury, Maryland.

"Hey, did we check if there were any calls from Fernanda Torres's phone to the DMV here in Virginia?"

"Umm, let me check."

He started rummaging through each file for the list of phone numbers. Like Ruby, he only found them in Averie and Daisy's files. Gabe looked at her, confused that they didn't have this information in Fran McCormick's file.

Ruby pulled up Fran McCormick's address and located the nearest DMV. It was in Charlottesville.

"Do you still have the list on your laptop?"

"Yeah. Pulling it up now. Okay, got it."

"Were there any calls to 804-497-7100?"

Gabe quickly typed in the number to the search and hit enter. Ruby slid her chair over next to him just in time to see the search load. Barely ten seconds had passed before six calls populated in the search.

"Son of a …" Gabe cursed to himself.

"Okay, so we know either Fernanda or the perp called the DMV local to each woman prior to the murders. What we don't know is why. Maybe they know someone that works there?"

"Wouldn't that mean they know someone at each branch in three different states?"

"Yeah … wait a second," Ruby said as she jumped up like she'd been stung by a bee. She rummaged through each file and pulled out the license information for each woman. She held up the pages to Gabe. "It's all here. Their height, weight, addresses, birthdays …"

The realization hit Ruby like a concrete beam. She was too stunned to speak.

"What? What is it?"

"Look …"

Ruby pointed to Fran McCormick's birthdate on her license and then to the homicide report. Gabe's eyes widened larger than cup saucers.

"He's killing them on their birthdays?"

Ruby pulled her chair back over to her desk and started typing all three dates into her browser to see if there was anything in common that happened on the dead women's birthdays. The search revealed only one thing that had happened on all three dates: a full moon.

"He's killing women whose birthdays are also the same day as a full moon."

"Ruby, when's the next full moon?"

She typed Gabe's question into the search bar and held her breath. Ruby gasped at the search results. "Tonight," she croaked out, horrified that they had merely a few hours to find the killer before he struck again. He could be anywhere in the country, and they had zero leads.

Gabe looked at his watch and then back at Ruby. "How are we going to do this by *tonight*?"

Ruby shook her head. As much as she wanted to tell him they'd get through it, they'd catch the guy in time and save the day, she could not. And something in her gut told her this might be their only chance to stop him. Ruby couldn't stomach another dead woman at the hands of this guy. If this unsub succeeded, she knew she'd have his next victim's blood on her hands too.

"I don't know, Gabe, but we have to try."

Gabe nodded. He was just as committed to solving this case as she was. She looked at the victims' files in front of her and back at her laptop screen.

"Hey, give me the time of death for Fran McCormick," Ruby said as she was typing on her laptop.

"Between midnight and one a.m."

"What about the other two?"

Gabe flipped through the pages in each file until he found what he needed. "Same."

"So, he's killing them right around the time the moon is at its apex."

"*Moonlight drowns out all but the brightest stars.*"

"Oh my god," Ruby gasped.

Ruby didn't actually want proof that the killer was one of Vallejo's devotees. But she now fully understood there were no coincidences with Vallejo. She didn't know how this unsub was connected to the Lucky 13 Killer, but she was going to find out, and she was going to do everything in her power to stop him. Stop *both* of them.

Serial killers are like weeds. You pull one up, two more sprout up in its place. The sickness, it spreads.

Ruby shut out her mother's words and focused on what they had figured out so far.

"We know he's killing women on their birthdays, which are also on the same days as full moons. We also know he contacted the DMV and got their information. But that doesn't make sense. No one can just call the DMV and get someone's personal information."

"What about if they work for the DMV?" Gabe asked with raised eyebrows.

"That's got to be it! He must be calling in and giving his employee ID or something to get the information. But that still seems off."

"Agreed. I don't think they just hand out all that information over the phone like that, not even if they could verify the guy. You saw how close-lipped they were with me."

"But you still got *some* information, which you then confirmed against what we already had."

"Right. So that means he's got to be pulling the names himself and then calling the local branch to confirm the information. That way, he doesn't risk raising as many red flags."

Ruby checked the time. They had less than twelve hours until the full moon was at its highest. They needed help if they were going to catch this guy in time.

CHAPTER TWENTY EIGHT

Ruby checked the time. Eight hours until the apex. Bellisario had pulled four additional agents to help them look through all the information based on their new lead. They had tried pulling a list of everyone whose birthday was that day, but that list was in the tens of thousands. Then Ruby had realized that the potential victim's birthday wasn't *that* day, but rather the next day, since he killed them after midnight.

They'd had to start over. A whole hour wasted, and they were no closer to anything concrete. Ruby went back to checking Fernanda Torres's contacts to see if any of them lived near one of the victims. So far, she had nothing. Just like everyone else.

Six hours until the apex.

Ruby looked at the numbers and then she looked at her laptop. There had to be an easier way to sort through everything and find this guy. Then, it hit her. *Milo Quincy.*

She quickly pulled up an internal chat box and messaged Milo. He was in green, so hopefully that meant he could help. Ruby chewed on her bottom lip as she waited for a response. Three dots popped up, indicating Milo was typing.

Hi there, Special Agent Hunter. What's up?

I need your help. Can I call you?

The three dots appeared again and then nothing. Ruby waited. The three dots appeared once more. Then her laptop started ringing, and Milo's face popped up on the screen asking to connect to a video call. She clicked the green phone icon.

"How can I help?" Milo asked.

"We're trying to narrow down our list of potential victims so we can find this guy, but it's got thousands of names on it. We're running out of time, so I figured I needed to call in the best."

"Flattery is always welcome, Special Agent Hunter. So, what do you have so far?"

"Hear me out. I was thinking that if the unsub works for the DMV, he likely looked up a list of women whose birthdays are tomorrow. Is that something you could search for?"

"Are you asking Milo or *Lil Mitnick*?"

Ruby smiled. "Who do you think?"

He smiled back as he started typing at what seemed like warp speed.

"What's the profile?"

"White male. Late twenties to early thirties. 6'3" or taller."

In less than a minute, Milo had something. "Okay, we have got six. No … make that three possible suspects."

"Is there any way to narrow it down further?"

"Already on it."

"If you were here, Milo, I'd kiss you! In an HR appropriate way of course."

"Of course. Okay, one of the guys is currently checked into a psychiatric hospital in California."

"Could he check himself out?"

"No, he's on a seventy-two-hour hold for a 5150."

"Okay, what about the other two?"

"The other two … are both off on PTO today and tomorrow. Their names are Evan Pearson and Frederick Linton. I am sending over their information now. However, the women they looked up are in opposite directions."

"What do you mean? Like in the same state?"

"Not even close. Evan Pearson looked up Natali Williams in Plantation View, Georgia. Frederick Linton looked up Janna Ericson in Pikeville, Michigan. I am sending their information over as well."

"Milo, you're an absolute genius."

"Thank you, Special Agent Hunter. Ping me if you need anything else. I'll keep an eye out," he said with a grin as the video chat closed.

"We've got something!" Ruby shouted to get the group's attention. Everyone, including Bellisario, looked up. "We have two possible suspects who looked up women with birthdays tomorrow … One of the women is in Michigan, and the other is in Georgia. We need agents on the ground in both places, and we've only got five and a half hours left."

"Special Agent Hunter, you go to Georgia, and Special Agent Ruiz you go to Michigan. Head out to the airport, and I'll have you both on flights by the time you get there," Bellisario said matter-of-factly. Ruby nodded and headed toward the elevator. Gabe was right on her heels.

*

Ruby messaged Milo from the car asking him to run the suspects' phone numbers. He messaged back that he'd send them the location information as soon as he had it.

"Milo's going to send you Frederick Linton's phone information, so you'll have it when you land."

"I don't like the idea of us splitting up, Ruby."

"Me either, but sometimes we have to do what we have to do."

"How long is your flight?"

"Two hours. And it looks like yours is an hour and forty-five minutes."

"At least we don't have to check bags or anything."

"Yeah."

Ruby's adrenaline was fighting her fatigue in a never-ending battle. She needed to be as alert as possible. Vallejo's followers were violent and quick to fight. Ruby could not afford to be tired. She guzzled the rest of the cold coffee she'd brought with her and made a note to get coffee on the plane.

She looked over at Gabe as he expertly weaved through traffic.

"What?"

"Nothing. I just … Do you think we're going to get there in time?"

"I hope so."

Ruby's phone pinged. Milo messaged over the phone numbers for both suspects.

"Milo sent us the phone numbers for both unsubs. I am going to start calling them now to see if I can get at least one of them on the phone. Maybe we can narrow it down further before we get to the airport."

Gabe nodded as he focused on the road. Ruby didn't know how fast they were going, but it felt like the lights of other cars were flying by in lines.

Ruby dialed the first number. It went straight to voicemail. She dialed the second number. It rang several times before going to voicemail. She tried the first number again. It rang twice and then went to voicemail. The number belonged to Evan Pearson. She tried Frederick Linton's number again, but it just rang and rang before going to voicemail like it had before.

"Is there anything else we can use to eliminate one of these guys?" Gabe asked while she continued trying Evan Pearson's number. Now, it wasn't even ringing; it was just going to voicemail. Ruby suspected by the pattern that Evan Pearson had his phone and was declining her call.

"The victims lived in towns that started with Ps. Janna Ericson is in Pikeville, Michigan."

"Then it's got to be her, right?"

"Natali Williams is in Plantation View, Georgia."

Gabe sighed loudly as she slumped back in her seat. It was like every time they'd seen a glimpse of the finish line ahead, it disappeared like a bad mirage.

Ruby tried calling Frederick Linton again. Once again, it just rang several times before going to voicemail.

"Milo emailed us info for both suspects as well as their potential victims. I'm going to see if he can send us a file for each with everything he can find before we board. We'll both have down time on the flight, so we might as well use it to our advantage."

"That's a good idea. Maybe he'll find something concrete that actually links one of the suspects to Vallejo."

"To be honest, I don't know if anything like that exists, Gabe. We have looked under every nook and cranny of the last two killers to see if we could find any kind of connection. Jared Reuben was the only one we know met Vallejo before we caught him. Aaron Rodney crawled out of the woodwork like a termite, and God knows how many more are under the boards."

"Maybe. But we have Milo Quincy on our side," Gabe smiled. Ruby half-smiled in return. She appreciated he was trying to see the positive in what seemed to be the most adverse of situations. It reminded her of Asher, and for once, she appreciated the memory.

Five minutes later, they arrived at the airport, the car barely in park before they had both jumped out of it and ran toward the doors. Two planes were waiting on standby just as Bellisario had said they would be.

"Don't die," Gabe said. Ruby guessed it was his version of "good luck."

"You either."

Thirty minutes later, they were both airborne.

Four hours until the apex.

CHAPTER TWENTY NINE

Once the plane stopped climbing, Ruby pulled out her laptop. She used her phone's secure hotspot to log on to the FBI server so she could check her email. Milo's email contained the files she'd asked for, including detailed information on the potential victim.

Ruby clicked on the file for Evan Pearson. A list of documents and image files appeared. She double-clicked on an image file. A few seconds later, she was staring at Evan Pearson's face. She wasn't sure why, but she was surprised at how clean-cut and normal he looked.

The man had dark brown hair that was high and tight on the sides and longer on top. It had some wave to it, which he parted on the side. Maybe keeping the sides short kept the waviness in control. His eyes looked like they were either a light brown or hazel, but Ruby could not tell from the picture. He was clean-shaven, had a strong English nose that looked like it had been broken a few times, and what looked like capped teeth. Ruby found it odd he'd pay thousands of dollars to fix his teeth but not fix his nose.

He looked like a guy from one of those rural towns Vallejo loved. He'd probably played football or some other team sport and was the big fish in his little pond. But something interrupted this guy's trajectory. Something other than Vincent Vallejo.

As Ruby stared at his photo, she realized he looked like just an ordinary guy. He wasn't menacing; he didn't sneer. He seemed affable almost, like someone you'd say hello to as you passed them by. Other than his sheer size, Evan Pearson wasn't at all what she pictured when she thought of this serial killer. Then again, neither was Ted Bundy.

Ruby closed the image file and clicked on one of the documents. Milo had pulled everything about Evan Pearson he could find in every database he could access.

Evan Pearson was born in a one stoplight, farm town south of DC. He was twenty-nine years old, had no siblings, and both of his parents were deceased. His father died when Evan was in high school in some kind of farm equipment accident. His mother was killed by a drunk driver his freshman year in college.

Ruby realized that was the hole in his story she was missing. Vallejo wasn't a god or a superhuman, but he was charming, and he knew how to spot a lost lamb a mile away. She suspected Evan Pearson was desperate for a father figure when he met Vallejo, and Vallejo was ready to start or had already started cultivating his flock.

Ruby continued reading Evan's filed and saw he'd almost flunked out of school during the first semester of his sophomore year. But by Christmas break, he was making straight A's.

Ruby wondered if his mother's death had triggered a spiral at the start of his sophomore year. It made sense if it had. What didn't make sense was that Ruby had never seen that kind of turn-around, certainly not without help.

Ruby looked up what college Evan had attended. Pine Mountain State College. Ruby felt like she'd heard that name before. She pinged Milo, asking him if he could find out if Vincent Vallejo had ever taught at Pine Mountain State College. She hit send, hoping it wouldn't take to long to hear back from him.

Vincent Vallejo had taught at several community and state colleges. He seemed to have trouble staying in one place for too long. Once they caught him, they had investigated every cold case from every town he had ever worked or lived in. Nothing turned up besides his attempted murder of Maureen Fantasia and the thirteen murders he was convicted for.

Ruby went back to Evan Pearson's file. He graduated magna cum laude with a degree in Criminal Justice, but he didn't have any additional educational pursuits. This unsub was definitely schooled in police procedures, but she wasn't sure he would have learned what he needed to know from his undergraduate studies. *No*, Ruby thought, *someone's trained him to be this good.*

Her phone vibrated with a response from Milo. Ruby scoured the list of schools Vallejo had taught, most of which were local community and technical colleges. And there it was, right in the middle of her list. Pine Mountain State College. Ruby checked the years he was teaching at the school and then she cross-referenced them to Evan Pearson's college years. They were a match.

Ruby hit forward and typed in Bellisario and Ruiz's emails. Before she hit send, she typed in a quick note that simply read: *Evan Pearson graduated from Pine Mountain State College when Vincent Vallejo was a professor there. Concrete link confirmed.*

Ruby continued trying to call Evan Pearson. She wasn't sure what she was going to do if she actually got him on the phone, but she had to try. Each time, it went straight to voicemail. She speculated that he'd likely blocked her by now. Especially if he was the killer. And at this point, Ruby was pretty sure Gabe's suspect was another misdirection, and Evan Pearson was their guy. The thought was sobering.

What if she didn't get there in time? What if she couldn't take him down by herself? What if he got away? Ruby could not help but play the "what if" game as if her life depended on it. In some ways, it did. Not just *her* life.

She closed Evan Pearson's file and double clicked on Natali Williams's file. The first thing she did once she got it open was locate the woman's phone number. She dialed the ten digits on her keypad and hit the green call key.

"Hello?"

"Hi, is this Natali Williams?"

"Oh, please take me off your call list. I am not interested in any products or services right now."

"I am not a telemarketer. My name is Special Agent Ruby Hunter, and I am with the FBI. Is this Natali Williams?"

"Oh my gosh, yes, so sorry. I can't stand telemarketers."

"Okay, where are you right now?"

"I am just getting home from work. You caught me just as I'm walking in the door. Why? What's going on?"

Ruby heard the door close in the background, and she was just about to explain why she was calling when Natali made a sound like something was off.

"Are you okay, Natali?"

"Yes, I just thought I'd locked the deadbolt this morning. That's strange."

"I need you to get out of your house right now, Natali. Get out of your house, get in your car, and drive to the nearest police station. Do you understand me?"

"Okay," the woman said, fear rising in her voice.

"Lock the doors as soon as you get in your car. Okay?"

"Okay."

Ruby listened to see if she could hear any background noises, to see if anyone was there with Natali. Maybe she'd gotten to Natali before Evan Pearson had. Seconds later, a scream of sheer terror rang out in Ruby's ear. She nearly dropped her phone it was so loud.

“Natali? Natali? Natali?” Ruby called out, but all she could hear was the sound of footsteps hitting pavement and more screams.

CHAPTER THIRTY

As soon as the plane came to a stop, Ruby was out of her seat and headed for the door. The flight attendant moved out of her way, wishing her luck as she rushed down the stairs. The black-and-white squad car was sitting about twenty feet away with a uniformed police officer leaning against it.

"Special Agent Hunter?"

"That's me. May I have the keys please?"

"I can take you wherever …"

"Give me the keys."

The officer handed them over and moved out of the way.

"Thank you," Ruby called out to him as she shut the car door, leaving the officer behind.

Ruby pinged Milo to call her as she plugged her phone into the car's dash. Not even five seconds later, Milo was talking to her through the car's intercom system.

"Their cell phones are both still hitting off the same towers in the area, so they could be at Natali's house or on the move. I've got you on satellite and can tell you where to go from here."

"Great. How far away am I from her house?"

"Four minutes."

Ruby started the engine and put the car in drive. She followed Milo's directions to the interstate, turning exactly where he told her to so she could get there quickly. He was better than any phone or car GPS, and far more accurate.

"I am so glad you know where I am going because I would have gotten stuck in that maze of an exit back there."

"I don't know why they always want to make it hard to leave the airport. You'd think they had made it harder for you to get in. Take the next exit."

Ruby did as she was told. He guided her through six green lights, which she assumed he had something to do with, and had her turn right two times before she entered Marsh Creek Commons. Newer single and two-story homes lined the streets, but it wasn't a cookie-cutter neighborhood.

"Turn left and it's the last house on the right before the trees. Blue two-story."

Thirty seconds later, Ruby put the police car in park.

"Don't hang up," she called to Milo as she jumped out of the car and ran up to the front porch. The front door was ajar, and a large, potted plant was turned over. Black, damp soil had spilled out everywhere.

"Natali? Natali? Are you here?" Ruby called out. No one responded. She listened for any crick or creak of the house to see if someone was upstairs. Ruby didn't know if he'd had the chance to strangle Natali, and she was already dead or what. She drew her gun and carefully side-stepped the dirt on the floor. She quietly walked through the house, checking every door, and hoping she wasn't going to find a body.

Ruby made her way upstairs, taking one step at a time and stopping to listen just to make sure she was alone. She checked each bedroom and both bathrooms upstairs. Natali wasn't there. No one was.

As Ruby started down the stairs, she noticed something she hadn't seen when she was going up the stairs a minute or so earlier. Directly across from the top step, a thick rope hung from a beam in the foyer of Natali's home. It was tucked into a curtain, but Ruby was pretty sure it was the killer's rope. She raced down the stairs and shook the curtain loose in order to free the rope without touching it. Sure enough, the thirteen-threaded rope dangled in front of her, confirming the killer had been lying in wait for Natali when she got home.

It looked like the killer was going to hang her instead of strangling her, which seemed odd to Ruby. Why deviate? Evan Pearson, who she was almost certain was the killer, had gone to great lengths to kill each woman the exact same way with pieces of rope all from the same source. She couldn't help but wonder what changed. Why now?

Ruby slammed shut the door behind her and hurried back to the running squad car.

"Milo, she's not here."

"It looks like wherever she is, she's with Evan. Let me see if I can pinpoint their location a little more precisely."

"I think Natali did what I said. I think she got to her car and drove out of here before he could get to her. Or at least I hope so."

"Then he's likely in pursuit because their phones are literally within fifteen feet of each other."

"Okay, let's put out an APB for any speeders in the area. You've got their car info right?"

"Already on it."

Ruby put on her seatbelt and put the car in drive. Just as she was pulling away from Natali's house, Milo got a hit.

"We've got a high-speed chase on the interstate near the house. A highway patrolman is in pursuit and called in the license plate information of the car he's behind. It's registered to Evan Pearson."

"What channel do I need to put this thing on to hear what's going on?"

"I've got it," Milo said. The police radio flipped to the channel the highway patrolman was using. He was calling for backup, a spike strip, anything to get the cars to stop before someone got killed. The patrolman's voice was frantic, young. Ruby worried he wasn't experienced enough to deal with the situation he'd found himself in.

"There are two of them, right? He's chasing her?"

"Yes," Milo confirmed. Ruby breathed the tiniest bit easier knowing Natali at least wasn't in the same vehicle as Evan Pearson. *Little victories.*

Ruby listened to the cop chatter as Milo guided her toward the pursuit. Then, she heard a series of gun shots ring out so close that they echoed in the background.

"Son of a …!" the cop on the radio shouted. Dispatch radioed the cop, but he didn't respond right away. Then, after a string of curse words he yelled, "He shot out my front tires! I am in the median, but I'm good. Just out of commission. I repeat, the second driver is armed."

"Turn right now. It'll get you on the interstate, and you'll only be three exits behind them."

Ruby yanked the steering wheel to the right, causing the tires to squeal. She pressed on the gas, hoping she still remembered the basics of pursuit driving and PIT maneuvers should she need it. As soon as she hit the exit ramp for the interstate, Ruby floored it. The car lurched forward, faster than she was ready for.

"You okay, Special Agent Hunter?"

"Yeah. Call me Ruby."

"Okay, Ruby, if you continue to accelerate, you should catch up to them in less than two minutes. It looks like there's some traffic up ahead."

"It's the middle of the night. Why are people out on the roads?"

"It's a Friday?"

“Ahh,” she said as she pushed the car’s speedometer higher and higher. Ruby could not remember the last time she’d gone out on a Friday night, much less stayed out past midnight. The darkness and headlights messed with her eyes, making it hard to focus on where she was going.

“You’ve got a wall of cop cars coming up behind you, and there are cops headed toward them on the other side. I have already let them know you’re a friendly because you’re going to get to them first. Evan Pearson is driving a white, two-door Honda CRV on the back. He’s chasing Natali in her silver, four-door Toyota Camry. They should be just up ahead. You ready?”

Ruby unsnapped her holster so she could grab her gun quickly if she needed it. She was a decent shot, but she hadn’t fired her weapon from a moving car in a long time. She also wasn’t sure if taking Evan Pearson out was the right thing to do, but as long as he was putting Natali Williams in harm’s way, Ruby was going to do what she had to do.

She pressed the gas pedal harder and focused her sights ahead.

“As ready as I am going to get.”

CHAPTER THIRTY ONE

The white Honda CRV came into view within ten seconds. Ruby looked at her speed, and the needle was pushing over 100 mph. She overheard the cops on the radio talking about how to safely get the two of them off the road, especially the Toyota Camry.

Milo coordinated with the police as Ruby caught up to Evan. He was right on Natali's bumper, edging closer and closer. Ruby managed to pull up almost as close to Evan's bumper, hoping to distract him. She flipped on the lights and sirens and started blaring her horn at him. Nothing worked. She kept up the noise and stayed on his bumper. She wasn't sure anything would make Evan Pearson give up his pursuit of Natali Williams.

Ruby was impressed that through it all, Natali appeared to be holding her own. She was weaving in and out of traffic, desperate to lose Evan. Ruby knew all too well that fear was often a great motivator for survival.

She kept the lights and sirens going as she got as close to Evan's backend as possible without hitting him. She hoped Natali saw someone was on his tail, too, that it would give her comfort to know she wasn't alone.

The good guys are on the way, Natali. Just hang in there.

Evan followed Natali's every swerve and maneuver, while Ruby followed Evan. The speed of the chase lessened as more cars came into play, but not the danger.

"You still with me, Milo?"

"Right here, Ruby."

"What do you know about PIT maneuvers?"

"I don't think that's a good idea. It doesn't sound like you've ever done one before, which means you're at a huge disadvantage. You're coming up on higher elevation and using a PIT maneuver could mean you both go through the railing unless you know what you're doing. Plus, it's dark, which is only going to make it harder for you to get help if you go through the rails."

Ruby had only ever seen a PIT maneuver, not performed one herself. PIT stood for Precision Immobilization Technique, and it was used in high-speed pursuits to force the fleeing car to abruptly turn 180 degrees. To do that, the police car typically bumped the left or right backend of the car with enough force that the driver would lose control and ultimately stop the vehicle.

The three cars continued to veer in and out of traffic like a fast-moving snake. Two cop cars trailed Ruby, but no one seemed to be able to get ahead of Evan.

"What's up ahead of us, Milo?"

"Heavier traffic. You're about to hit that low shoulder area I was talking about, Ruby. If you don't pull off the PIT maneuver just right, you're going straight through those guard rails. It's a steep slope through a lot of trees, and your chance of survival is drastically reduced."

Ruby considered what Milo told her and looked up ahead. Evan Pearson wasn't stopping, and no one seemed to be able to get between him and Natali Williams. Ruby was the only one close enough to potentially stop or at least divert him from trailing Natali, which could end up being deadly for both of them.

"I need you to get emergency services out here. Fire, medical, everything."

"You know I can disable your car, right?"

"I am not going to let him win, Milo. Natali Williams is not going to die today. Make the call."

"I'm sending everyone your way, but if you do this, I don't know how long it'll take to get you help down in a ravine. Can you hold your own with this guy long enough if you have to?"

"I guess we'll find out."

Ruby quickly jerked the car into the right lane so she could get in position next to Evan's right backend. She pressed on the gas pedal and braced for impact. As soon as the front end of the squad car was just past his right rear wheel, Ruby yanked the car to the left as hard as she could and slammed into the CRV.

For a moment, everything seemed like it was stuck in slow motion. Evan Pearson's CRV spun around until the other side was parallel to her as she lunged forward toward the guard railing. She was going over, and it looked like he was coming with her. Ruby looked right at Evan Pearson. His face was contorted with rage and shock that she'd intervened. Ruby gave him her biggest, proudest smile as she tore through the metal railing and plunged down the side of the embankment.

She was going so fast down the hill that she could barely avoid hitting a tree. Ruby wasn't sure how she was going to get the car to stop. She looked in her rearview mirror and saw the CRV rolling down after her. This was bad. Even if she did get the car to stop without hitting anything, Evan Pearson's car was going to ram right into her.

"Evan's car is rolling toward me, Milo. We're going to crash!" Ruby shouted as she cut the wheel to the left and smashed the tail end of the black and white into a tree. She heard a loud boom as the squad car made contact and then the scraping sound of metal-on-metal as Evan Pearson's CRV slammed into her.

"Ruby? Ruby? Can you hear me?"

Ruby could hear Milo's worried tone, but she could not make out what he was saying. He sounded so far away, like the intercom had been pulled out of the car and carried off into the distance.

She tried to move, but every attempt was met with sharp, searing pain. Ruby struggled to respond to Milo, but she could not get the words to form properly in her mouth. All she could do was groan as the lights and sirens of the car seemed to fade. Black specks multiplied in her vision until she slipped away into the darkness.

CHAPTER THIRTY TWO

Ruby's eyes flew open as she desperately grasped for air. Her throat was being crushed by something, what she didn't know. She reached up to her neck to feel what was happening. A thick rope cut into her skin and snuffed out her air. She could not even scream.

A heavy weight bore down on her back, a boulder crushing her into the ground. Evan. She could hear the sound of his breathing. Now, she was on the ground. Somehow, he'd dragged her from the car.

He pulled the rope tighter as Ruby scratched and grabbed at it, frantic to get free. Her vision started to get spotty, and she knew she didn't have much time before the lack of oxygen was going to knock her out.

Ruby mustered every bit of strength she had to push herself off the ground. The weight on her back wobbled, giving her just enough room to swing her elbow back as hard as she could. It made contact with bone, and the rope around her neck loosened. She snatched it from around her neck, sucking in as much air as possible.

Ruby looked back just in time to see Evan Pearson barreling toward her out of the darkness. She quickly rolled to the side and, using his own weight against him, shoved him straight into a tree. She had to get to her feet. She knew if she didn't, he was going to get that rope wrapped around her throat again. Ruby knew that would be it for her.

She scrambled to her feet and turned toward the assailant. He was unrelenting. He bore down on her with death in his eyes. Ruby grabbed a piece of metal and hurled it at Evan Pearson. It nicked his arm as he blocked it, doing a lot less damage than Ruby had hoped.

He sprung forward, but Ruby dove out of the way. She quickly got to her feet and looked for something, anything, she could use as a weapon. Mangled car parts were strewn about from the crash. There had to be something.

Ruby did her best to keep a safe distance between her and Evan, but he was closing in fast. The only thing she could think to do was run. She leapt over a blown-out tire and took off toward the embankment.

If only I could get back up to the road, she thought.

Evan's car was the only obstacle between her and freedom, and it was engulfed in flames from the crash. There was no way she was going to be able to escape Evan by running. She was going to have to defend herself and hope she could do it long enough until help arrived.

Ruby circled back on Evan, which surprised him. It was like he was counting on the chase. Ruby watched Evan, but she also kept an eye out for where she was going. They circled each other like two wild animals. Ruby decided on an offensive approach. Evan's three victims had all died with him behind them. If he was going to kill her, he was going to look her in the eyes when he did it.

Ruby quickly pulled her belt off and whipped the buckle end toward his head. It caught him just above the eye, forcing him backwards. She stepped into him and whacked him again, this time in the jaw. Ruby didn't stop. She lashed the belt at him over and over as he tried to fight it off.

Evan Pearson was not used to being on the receiving end of pain. He backed away with his arms taking the brunt of the whipping, a weak attempt to protect his head from further injury. Ruby had lost control. She was thrashing the belt at him over and over, a sort of bloodthirst taking over. He would not win. *Vallejo* would not win.

Ruby continued her assault on Evan, which wasn't doing as much damage as she'd hoped. As she raged forward, he tripped backwards over a burning tire. The entire area had caught on fire from the crash, and Evan was now flat on his back, surrounded by flames.

Ruby thought about who Evan was when Vallejo first met him. Orphaned by the death of his parents, Vallejo took him in and showed him the way. Like some sort of father-figure. Ruby realized Vallejo saw in Evan what he didn't have—a legacy.

This one isn't like the other two. Vallejo made sure of that.

Fernanda Torres's words came back to her in a rush, and finally she understood how to get Evan to surrender. She held the belt to her side, ready to strike if her words failed.

"In the grand scheme of things, Evan, you don't matter. No one is going to remember you or what you did here. No one even knows you're connected to Vincent Vallejo. *He's the one* the world is going to remember. *Lucky 13*. You're just a pawn in his chess game, nothing more."

"You don't know what you're talking about!" Evan argued as he started to get up. Ruby raised her arm with the belt, ready to strike.

"If you even try to get up, I'll beat you senseless."

He stilled, but he didn't surrender. His hands clenched into fists, ready to strike.

"I know you're smart enough to know better. I saw your grades and all you achieved. *You* did that, Evan. *Not him*."

"He saved me. Without him, I would have ended up dead in an alley somewhere."

"Maybe. But saints don't hold sins against sinners. He's just a man, Evan. He's just a man who saw a troubled boy he could mold into someone like him."

"Then he succeeded because I am just like him," Evan snarled, some fight still left in him.

"If you can't see how he's used you to strengthen his own legacy, then, no, Evan, you're not like him. He'd be smart enough to see that coming from a mile away."

"How would you know?"

"Do you know how we figured out your victims were connected? *He* told us."

"That's not true."

"It absolutely is. I interviewed him, myself, and he gave us the information we needed to connect the murder of Fran McCormick to Daisy Hauser. Had he not done that, we wouldn't have known how to find you. We wouldn't have been able to stop you from killing Natali. *He* gave you up like just another pawn in his game."

Ruby could see the wheels turning in Evan's mind. He was weighing what he knew about Vallejo with everything she'd told him. She wasn't sure which way he was going to go, but she was ready to beat the mess out of him to survive, adrenaline pulsating through her.

"Per lunam ad astra." The words were defiant, his pledge of allegiance to Vallejo. He was letting her know that he was willing to die for the cause. Ruby wasn't interested in killing him. She wanted him alive to show Vallejo she could beat him at his own game.

"What did he tell you that means, Evan?"

"'Through the moon to the stars.' We are all stars in his universe, Special Agent Hunter. Even *you*."

"Well, my Latin is a little rusty, but that saying has multiple meanings. What you said sounds right, but it could also mean '*by* the moon *among* the stars.' By his light you will be among the stars. Don't you see? There are billions of stars, Evan, but only one moon. At least on this planet."

Evan shook his head in disbelief. She could tell she'd gotten through to him. She'd planted the seed of doubt, and it was growing rapidly. Ruby lowered her arm, anticipating his surrender.

"Evan Pearson, you are under arrest. I want you to slowly stand up and put your hands on your head."

Evan didn't respond. Ruby backed up a little, unsure of what his next move would be. She didn't have much more fight in her, but she hoped he'd do the right thing and do as he was told.

A moment later, Evan jumped to his feet and launched himself at her, one last attempt to take her down. She quickly moved out of his way, and with all of her might, swung the belt as hard as she could at his head. The *thwack* was more satisfying than she'd expected.

The stars must've aligned for Ruby because Evan finally collapsed, semi-conscious from the blow. She sprinted to the squad car for handcuffs and returned quickly enough to thwart his attempts to get up.

Ruby yanked his arms behind his back, cuffing his hands tightly, earning a sharp wail as she did so. She said his Miranda Rights and moved away from him just as the calvary arrived. Ruby's survival mode waned, and she crumbled to the ground from all the injuries she'd sustained. The next thing she knew, she was being rolled onto a stretcher and secured for transport.

"Someone tell Special Agent Ruiz we got him," she mumbled before passing out.

CHAPTER THIRTY THREE

There are still consequences for interfering with my legacy. Or maybe you're part of it. We'll let the biographers decide.

Vallejo's words snapped Ruby awake only to be met with the agony of several broken ribs, a broken collar bone, and a throat so swollen she wasn't sure how she'd been able to talk Evan Pearson down.

"Hang tight, Ruby. I'll get the nurse."

Ruby recognized the voice, but she could not place it. Her head felt too heavy to hold up, but something was helping her. She tried to feel what, but it hurt too badly to move. There were parts of her that hurt that she didn't even know she had.

"Ruby? Can you hear me?" a woman in purple scrubs asked.

She tried to answer the woman, who she assumed was the nurse the voice just told her that they were going to go get. Nothing except guttural croaks came out.

"Don't try to talk. Your vocal cords are bruised and swollen. It's going to be a little while before you can talk normally."

Ruby gave the nurse a dirty look. The woman shouldn't ask people questions if she knows they physically can't answer them.

"Ruby ..." the voice from earlier said, almost as if it was scolding her. She blinked her eyes a few times. They were so sore and sensitive to light.

"You're going to have a lot of aches and pains over the next few weeks. Between the car crash and the strangulation, you're a very lucky woman, Ruby Hunter," the nurse explained. Then she told the other person in the room that she'd be right outside. She also suggested closing the blinds some to help Ruby's eyes adjust.

The shadowy figure moved from her bed to the window in two steps. She heard the blinds flip closed with a snap. Ruby blinked her eyes a few times, trying to make them focus.

"Take your time," the voice said.

Ruby recognized the voice, but who it belonged to still wasn't registering. Her brain felt so scrambled. She wondered if she had permanent damage from Evan's assault.

"Can you see me, Ruby?" the voice asked. Ruby blinked a few more times and tried to adjust her head to see the person better. White hot pain enveloped her neck, forcing her to cry out.

"It's okay, it's okay. I'll get the nurse to help manage your pain. All right? I'll be here when you wake up."

A minute later, Ruby felt warmth flood her body as she drifted off into nothing.

*

Flashes of the trees coming at Ruby at warp speed rushed back into her mind as the blanket of pain meds slowly lifted away. She jerked awake, terrified that she was back in the woods and Evan was coming for her. Every muscle throbbed like they were torn apart and never going to mend.

"Easy, Ruby."

There was that voice again. Ruby blinked a few times to see if she could make the shadowy figure come into focus. As it did, Ruby thought for just a moment that it was Asher Carnes.

"Asher?" she pushed out from her mangled voice box. It wasn't more than a whisper. Tears pooled in her eyes, blurring the figure enough where she could not tell if it was Asher or a perfect stranger.

Ruby felt warmth embrace her right hand and realized someone was holding her hand. Oh how desperately she wanted it to be Asher.

"I am so sorry, Ruby. It's me, Gabe."

Tears flowed freely from her eyes and down the sides of her face as she processed Asher's death all over again. It wasn't fair. She wondered why someone like Vincent Vallejo was still living and breathing, but Asher was in a box in the ground.

It was only a matter of minutes before the tears became full-blown weeping. It hurt to cry, but it also hurt to hold it in. She'd tried for so long to shove her feelings for Asher and what Vallejo had done to him down so far that she could not ever feel them again. Ruby thought she'd managed pretty well, but she was wrong.

Vallejo had tortured Asher so horribly that no one could bear to look Ruby in the eyes. She'd seen it, and those images of her murdered partner and lover were seared into her brain forever. Even at the trial, they didn't talk about Asher's injuries. They had only said they were "gruesome" and "inspired by the crucifixion." It wasn't something anyone wanted to relive, but Ruby felt like she relived it every day.

She woke up every morning thinking Asher would be lying in bed next to her. Instead, it was like waking up that morning with the bed cold and empty next to her. The sound of her phone vibrating had stirred her from sleep. At the time, she thought it was Asher texting her to meet him for breakfast or asking her what she wanted for breakfast. But it wasn't. By then, Asher had succumbed to his wounds. Vallejo had waited to text where Asher was. He never meant for Ruby to find her lover alive.

Ruby was too tired and too banged up to try and stop crying, even in front of Gabriel Ruiz. She let herself cry, full-on sob even, for the first time since Asher Carnes's murder. Gabe let her get it out, holding her hand the entire time.

Once Ruby regained her composure, Gabe filled her in on everything that had happened since the crash.

Unlike Jared Reuben, Evan Pearson was cooperating with authorities. He'd pleaded guilty without hesitation to three counts of murder, two counts of attempted murder, and several other charges. Most importantly, though, Natali Williams was alive, safe, and she wouldn't have to testify.

Ruby was right about Evan Pearson. He'd developed a nasty and very expensive drug habit after his mom died, which got him in trouble with the kind of people who bury bodies in the desert. Vallejo helped him. He paid his debt. He helped him get sober. He even tutored him so he could get back on track with his classes.

Evan had lived with Vallejo for three years, which was plenty of time for him to warp his impressionable mind. Evan never had a chance. Ruby wondered how many other Evans, Jareds, or Aarons there were out there, waiting to do Vallejo's bidding. She wasn't sure if it was ever going to end. Maybe this was her life now.

Ruby looked at Gabe and gave him a small smile, which was all she could manage at the moment. He'd stuck with her through the case and all but promised he wasn't going anywhere. She didn't realize at the time how much she'd needed him to reassure her he wasn't going to leave like all the others. He had her back, and she could trust that one hundred percent.

One of the benefits Ruby discovered of almost being strangled to death by a deranged serial killer was that Barrett Murphy finally cut her some slack. She was a hero, after all. Or at least for that day anyway.

"Yeah, Bellisario totally pulled rank on him and let him have it. In front of *everybody*. We were stunned to hear Warren Bellisario read

Murphy the riot act like that. I wish you could have seen it, Ruby. I thought about trying to record it, but I also like my job. I can't exactly be your partner if I get fired, now can I?"

Ruby smiled wider, even though it hurt so much more.

"All right, sir, it's time for the patient to get some rest," a woman in bright pink scrubs said as she entered Ruby's room.

"No problem," he said to the nurse as he stood up to go. Then he leaned over to Ruby's right ear and whispered, "When you get out of here and feel up to it, Hunter, let's go to Casa Comida's for lunch when we can actually sit and enjoy it. Deal?"

Ruby gave Gabe the slightest, almost imperceptible nod. He squeezed her hand and told her he'd be back in a little while.

It'd been a long time since Ruby had let anyone in. She'd thought that's what she needed to do in order to keep the people she cared about safe. *No attachments.* But that wasn't true. All having no attachments in her life did was make her lonely, miserable, and terrified of living her life. She'd seen the absolute worst in humanity through Vallejo. But she'd also seen the good, too, thanks to Asher, Bellisario, and Gabe.

Ruby understood as she lay in a hospital bed, broken bones and all, that she didn't have to do it all by herself anymore, and that felt really good. She wasn't sure if her epiphany filled her with comfort or the pain meds were kicking in, but Ruby allowed herself to let go of everything she'd been carrying for more than three years and finally live.

EPILOGUE

Two weeks later, Ruby clicked on the video chat icon of the internal messaging system to call Milo on her laptop. She figured the least she could do was talk to him face-to-face. She owed him a lot more, like several dozen apologies and thank yous.

"Look who it is!" Milo's grin was so wide it almost split his face in two with joy. "How are you feeling?"

"Better. I'm healing. I am so sorry, Milo, for not calling sooner. To be fair, I didn't actually start getting my voice back until this week."

"Is that all you're sorry for, Ruby?" he asked, still grinning.

"No, Milo, that's not all. I don't have the words right now to express how sorry I am or how thankful I am for dragging you into this mess."

"Those words sound pretty good to me."

Ruby could not keep from smiling. Milo Quincy was every bit the lovely man Asher had told her he was, and she was so grateful he was one of the "good guys."

"So, I heard that Lil Mitnick has some intel for me. Is he available?"

"For you, Ruby? Any day of the week."

Ruby's voice still wasn't fully back to normal several weeks later, but at least she didn't have to walk around with a white board anymore. She cleared her throat. "Okay, so lay it on me."

"Well, you know Gabe interviewed Evan and got some information, and I was able to extract some messages he might've sent to someone that has contact at Boone Correctional Facility."

She shifted. She'd read the transcript of their interview a thousand times. Evan said there was someone at the prison who helped get Vallejo's messages out once they had cut off all communications. Evan didn't know who it was, or if they were a guard, some other member of personnel, or another inmate.

"Okay, do we have a name?"

"No. But we have initials. H.S."

Initials. H.S. It wasn't a lot, but it was something. More than they'd had in a long time. "Thanks."

She ended the call, almost too abruptly, cringing when she cut him off as he attempted to say something.

Ruby picked up the phone on her desk and called Warden Percy Woodward. Now, more than ever, she wanted to find who was helping Vallejo and put a stop to this madness. Whatever brutal legacy he was hoping to create, she wanted to crush it, and do everything possible to erase Vallejo's name from the public consciousness—and her own mind—forever.

NOW AVAILABLE!

IF I FORGET

(A Ruby Hunter Mystery—Book 4)

FBI BAU Special Agent Ruby Hunter remains haunted by "The 13 Killer," the serial killer who took everything from her—including her partner—before she put him away for good. Yet somehow, though behind bars, new bodies are showing up with his trademark 13 signature. Is he behind it?

"Molly Black has written a taut thriller that will keep you on the edge of your seat… I absolutely loved this book and can't wait to read the next book in the series!"
—Reader review for Girl One: Murder

IF I FORGET is book #4 in a new series by #1 bestselling mystery and suspense author Molly Black, whose books have received over 2,000 five-star reviews and ratings.

A new serial killer is taking victims in seemingly random fashion—yet, somehow, Ruby feels they all are connected to the number 13.

Ruby races to crack the code, to figure out his M.O., before the next victim is claimed.

Yet the shocking twist is something not even Ruby can anticipate.

A complex psychological crime thriller full of twists and turns and packed with heart-pounding suspense, the RUBY HUNTER mystery series will make you fall in love with a brilliant new female protagonist and keep you turning pages late into the night.

Book #5—IF I RETURN—is also available.

Molly Black

Bestselling author Molly Black is author of the MAYA GRAY FBI suspense thriller series, comprising nine books (and counting); of the RYLIE WOLF FBI suspense thriller series, comprising six books; of the TAYLOR SAGE FBI suspense thriller series, comprising eight books; of the KATIE WINTER FBI suspense thriller series, comprising eleven books (and counting); of the RUBY HUNTER FBI suspense thriller series, comprising five books (and counting); of the CAITLIN DARE FBI suspense thriller series, comprising five books (and counting); and of the REESE LINK mystery series, comprising five books (and counting).

An avid reader and lifelong fan of the mystery and thriller genres, Molly loves to hear from you, so please feel free to visit www.mollyblackauthor.com to learn more and stay in touch.

BOOKS BY MOLLY BLACK

MAYA GRAY MYSTERY SERIES
GIRL ONE: MURDER (Book #1)
GIRL TWO: TAKEN (Book #2)
GIRL THREE: TRAPPED (Book #3)
GIRL FOUR: LURED (Book #4)
GIRL FIVE: BOUND (Book #5)
GIRL SIX: FORSAKEN (Book #6)
GIRL SEVEN: CRAVED (Book #7)
GIRL EIGHT: HUNTED (Book #8)
GIRL NINE: GONE (Book #9)

RYLIE WOLF FBI SUSPENSE THRILLER
FOUND YOU (Book #1)
CAUGHT YOU (Book #2)
SEE YOU (Book #3)
WANT YOU (Book #4)
TAKE YOU (Book #5)
DARE YOU (Book #6)

TAYLOR SAGE FBI SUSPENSE THRILLER
DON'T LOOK (Book #1)
DON'T BREATHE (Book #2)
DON'T RUN (Book #3)
DON'T FLINCH (Book #4)
DON'T REMEMBER (Book #5)
DON'T TELL (Book #6)

KATIE WINTER FBI SUSPENSE THRILLER
SAVE ME (Book #1)
REACH ME (Book #2)
HIDE ME (Book #3)

BELIEVE ME (Book #4)
HELP ME (Book #5)
FORGET ME (Book #6)
HOLD ME (Book #7)
PROTECT ME (Book #8)
REMEMBER ME (Book #9)
CATCH ME (Book #10)
WATCH ME (Book #11)

RUBY HUNTER FBI SUSPENSE THRILLER
IF I RUN (Book #1)
IF I TELL (Book #2)
IF I LIVE (Book #3)
IF I FORGET (Book #4)
IF I RETURN (Book #5)

CAITLIN DARE FBI SUSPENSE THRILLER
COME GET ME (Book #1)
COME FIND ME (Book #2)
COME TAKE ME (Book #3)
COME CATCH ME (Book #4)
COME SAVE ME (Book #5)

REESE LINK MYSTERY
BEYOND REASON (Book #1)
BEYOND REACH (Book #2)
BEYOND REPAIR (Book #3)
BEYOND DOUBT (Book #4)
BEYOND NORMAL (Book #5)

Made in the USA
Monee, IL
14 January 2025

76911768R00085